Blue Sky
STUDIOS

SPIES IN DISGUISE

THE JUNIOR NOVEL

Adapted by
Alexandra West
& Jim McCann

HARPER
An Imprint of HarperCollinsPublishers

Spies in Disguise: The Junior Novel
Spies in Disguise™ & © 2019 Twentieth Century Fox Film Corporation. All Rights
Reserved.
Printed in the United States of America.

www.harpercollinschildrens.com
Library of Congress Control Number: 2019950287
ISBN 978-0-06-285300-4
19 20 21 22 23   PC/BRR   10 9 8 7 6 5 4 3 2 1
❖
First Edition

CHAPTER
1
THE PROMISE

TICKTOCK, TICKTOCK . . . a timer counted down with precise accuracy.

"C'mon," a small voice said. The boy's tiny hand wiped sweat from his forehead, then went back to fitting steel tubes onto the metallic bands of a dime-store watch. Quickly, the screws spun into place as the screwdriver did its job.

"Caaaaarrrrefulll . . . Careful." The boy's voice shook slightly as his hands delicately threaded wires through the tubes and beads. Then, with just a moment's hesitation, he clipped the wire.

Reaching behind him, he pulled out an inflatable life jacket. Then, as if he was performing surgery, he used tweezers to gently lift the CO_2

cartridge out. At that crucial moment, he heard something.

"Walter Beckett, have you seen my twee-zers?"

The sudden sound startled Walter, who squeezed the CO_2 cartridge, causing it to go fly-ing straight at her, shattering her coffee mug. His mom, wearing her police uniform, gave Walter the kind of patient look only a mother can bestow on her young son.

"Umm, sorry, Mom. Did you need that mug?" Walter asked as the last of the coffee dripped from the broken bottom.

"What I needed was the coffee *inside* the mug," Wendy Beckett muttered before turning back to the true light of her life, her eight-year-old son, Walter, with his brown mop of hair covering his head, which seemed a little too big for his body.

He'll grow into that big brain of his one day, Wendy often thought.

She sat down opposite him, tossing the

broken pieces of the mug into the trash. The room was filled with gadgets and tubes and discarded items Walter swore he could turn into scientific treasures that would one day change the world. Wendy never discouraged him, and made sure he had everything he needed—as long as it was safe, of course.

"So, whatcha making, bud?"

Walter's eyes grew large and stayed that way even as he pulled up his goggles, which snapped him on the forehead. "I'm glad you asked, because it's for *you*!"

"Me?"

Walter nodded. "A gadget for you to wear on patrol."

Wendy leaned in closer as her son grew more excited.

"It's the perfect tool to keep you safe. Wanna see?" Wendy nodded as her son pulled out what appeared to be a mash-up of a watch and a bracelet, covered in buttons, that would cover half her forearm if she wore it. Walter launched into his presentation. "This button makes a really loud sound to incapacitate your enemy." He presses the button, and a high-pitched sound caused mother and son to cover their ears.

"Eeeeeeeoooooowwaaaaaaa!!!" Walter exclaimed, switching off the contraption.

He caught his breath and turned back to his mom. "Like that."

"Just like that would do the trick," Wendy said a little louder than normal, her ears still ringing.

"This button will wrap you in an inflatable hug so nobody can hurt you. I'll let you try that out later. But *this* one . . ." His eyes widened as far as they could go, as did his smile, revealing his masterpiece. "This is for when you're outnumbered. You just hold up your hand and say 'Stop!' and BOOM! Glitter cloud!" Walter said, his voice lowered in awe. "And the bad guys will leave you alone."

Wendy paused, then realized where her son's train of thought had led him. "Oh! Because glitter makes people happy?"

Walter looked at her, brow furrowed. "Because the refracted light causes the entero-chromaffin cells to release serotonin—" He saw his mother was not understanding. He sighed. "Yeah, glitter makes people happy."

An idea popped into his head. "Let's try it out! Remember how you told me not to take apart your cell phone?"

Wendy eyed her destroyed cell phone on her son's workshop table. "Not again! Come on, I—"

Glitter exploded everywhere, covering mother and son in sparkles. Walter flashed a smile, his eyes wide and expectant. "Still want to kill me?"

There was a moment before Wendy cracked, smiling and bringing her son in close, rubbing his hair and causing a glitter shower. "No. Just the opposite."

Walter had already begun spouting out ways to improve his gadget. "It worked! Next I want to add kitten visuals. No one can resist that com-bination!"

There was a brief buzz of static before police

dispatch called in for multiple police officers, including "Beckett, Wendy."

"That's me, hon. Time for my shift." She kissed him on the forehead and headed for the door. "Be good for Gram, okay?"

Walter grabbed a nearby backpack and the gadget and ran after his mom. "I'll come with you. I can finish this on the way. You won't even know I'm there. . . ."

"What you need to do is get ready for school."

Walter flopped in front of his mom, twirling the gadget in one hand absentmindedly. "Ughhh, Mom, school's boring and the kids think I'm weird."

"'Weird?' Hey, look at me." Wendy knelt down, facing her son. "What's wrong with weird? The world needs weird." Walter gave a slight smile.

Taking the gadget from her son's hand, Wendy continued. "Listen, I'm out there keeping the neighborhood safe. But one day, your ideas . . . your *gadgets* are gonna keep the world safe. And everybody will wish they were as weird as you."

"You think?" Walter whispered.

"I know," Wendy said, leaning in close. "Just promise me you will never give up.

Walter saluted. "Promise."

Smiling, Wendy outstretched her arms. "Good. Now give me a non-inflatable hug. Love you, partner," she said as they embraced. She pulled back and looked at Walter. "I promise I'll always have your back."

Wendy then took his watch and slipped it onto her wrist. "Team Weird?"

Walter smiled. "Team Weird."

CHAPTER
2
PLEASED TO MEET ME

FOURTEEN YEARS LATER

It was a snowy night in the mountains of Japan. Alongside one such mountain was a pagoda. The pagoda's four-sided stacked eaves rose three stories and lit the night sky. Two Yakuza guards—the 'Japanese mafia'—were patrolling . . . and whining to each other about the cold.

"Man, I agree!" A voice surprised them both. "It is COLD!"

The Yakuza guards turned their weapons on Special Agent Lance Sterling, the world's top superspy, dressed in his signature tuxedo. He

8

raised his hand to his head in a mock salute to his perfect dark hair.

"Hey, fellas. Konnichiwa. How you livin'?"

Both guards shook their weapons and began yelling in Japanese at once.

"Whoa, okay, okay. Everybody good? Be chill, like that snowman over there. See him? In just a minute, he's gonna be holding both your guns and we'll all be laughing. Then I'm gonna knock you both out."

The guards looked over at a snowman that absolutely was not there a moment ago. They looked at each other, then to Agent Sterling, but Lance was gone.

"Yoo-hoo," Lance called. He was standing by the snowman. In a flash, he whizzed to the guards and, with a flying chop, sent one guard's gun soaring into the snowman. A quick side kick to the other Yakuza and that guard's gun was in the snowman's other arm.

"Ha-ha! See? How fun was that?" Lance looked at the guards, then knocked their heads together and they fell. As he was stepping away, Lance heard a SPLAT and looked to find pigeons flying from the pagoda, and one had pooped on a guard's head.

Screwing up his face in disgust, Lance said, "Ugh, you did not deserve that. Rats with wings, I say." He then put on high-tech spy glasses, then activated his communicator and spoke into it. "I'm in position."

Back in the control room, screens lit up everywhere showing Lance's location: maps, infrared, POV visuals, everything to help guide the Agency's greatest asset as he carried out his mission.

"Whatcha got for me, Joyless?" Lance was the only person brave enough to call the director that to her face.

"You know I hate it when you call me that," she quipped back.

"That's what makes the job fun." Lance removed three buttons from his suit jacket and tossed them in the air to reveal they were tiny drones. The mini-aircraft buzzed around to send back a better image of Lance's surroundings.

"What is your situation?" Director Jenkins asked.

"Just getting visual now."

Something in the video feed from one of the drones caught the director's eye. "Tighter on that one, ten o'clock."

Using his high-tech spy glasses, Lance followed where she had guided him. With the touch of a button, he zoomed in on the image, revealing a massive mountain of a man, seated at a table, eating probably his fourth dinner of the day.

"Katsu Kimura," Lance sighed, recognizing him. "Everybody's favorite arms dealer."

Through his communicator, Lance could hear Joyless's gasp, and he imagined her pointing at the screen. "There! That briefcase is your objective."

Lance adjusted his goggles to zoom in tighter and saw a titanium briefcase on the table near Kimura. "Looks easy enough."

The director's voice was grave as she paced in the Control Room. "Inside is the M-9 Assassin, the first semi-autonomous attack drone." As she spoke, images of the Assassin in action played on screens around the room and were beamed to Lance's goggles for him to see as well. "It's powered by atmospheric energy. Never shuts down. Never stops pursuing its target."

"So it's an unstoppable killer robot that thinks for itself. Awesome! Maybe we should make one of those," Lance said sarcastically.

"We did," sighed the director. "That one is it. They stole it from our covert weapons lab."

As Lance watched Kimura, one of his flying buttons was picking up on something else. Just then, Drone Three's feed lit up, the screen filled with Yakuza guards rushing the pagoda's exterior. The agent monitoring Drone Three spoke up. "Director Jenkins, uhhh, he's got incoming." She pointed to the screen. "I'm detecting seventy extra hostiles around the perimeter."

Jenkins pinched her nose and squeezed her

eyes closed. Tough calls like this were why they made her director. "Ugh. I don't want another mess like Kyrgyzstan," she muttered. She took another look at the screen before she called it.

"Lance, listen," the superspy heard Director Jenkins say over his communicator. "You've got seventy Yakuza incoming. Stand down."

A grin flashed on the ace spy's face. "That's better odds than I usually get. Now or never, Joy."

"No, do not engage!" Director Jenkins commanded. "This time you need to wait for the backup team."

"Team?" Lance said, waving at one of the drones. "It's like you don't even know me. I fly solo."

With that, all three drones returned to Lance's hand. Joy paled, afraid of what he was about to do, knowing he was going to anyway.

"Wait! Lance, listen to me." But it was too late.

Lance had cut the feed from the drones and his communicator. The control room was filled with screens of nothing but snowy static.

Inside the pagoda, the Yakuza milled around in the common area. Some sharpened swords, others played cards, while more practiced the ancient art of gambling. In the middle of their lair was a giant fifty-thousand-gallon fish tank, filled with exotic fish, fake castles, and . . .

Agent Lance Sterling in a high-tech wet suit, observing everything.

He spotted Kimura, and—more importantly—the briefcase. As a plan formed in his mind, his thoughts were interrupted by the sound of a loud PING and a red blip appeared on one of Kimura's security screens.

Kimura immediately stood, directing his Yakuza lackeys. "The buyer is here! Go!"

The Yakuza all leaped into action mode. Two rushed out to meet "the buyer." Somehow, in all the chaos, no one managed to notice Lance in the fish tank.

"Huh," he said. Clearly Lance wasn't expecting anyone else to show up to this shindig. "Plot twist."

Outside, the two Yakuza watched as a sleek helicopter touched down on the snowy mountain. As soon as it landed, a tall, thin man exited, the kind that made the Yakuza grip their weapons in fear. Even more frightening was the menacing robotic left hand he flexed as he walked by, ignoring their bows. He marched into the pagoda as though he owned it.

Inside, even Kimura nodded, muttering "Killian," as the rest of his Yakuza quickly cleared a path for the man.

Killian stood at the opposite side of the long table from Kimura. He reached into his jacket and effortlessly slid a bulging silk bag across the table. Kimura plucked a diamond out of the bag and examined it. Satisfied, the large man slid the briefcase containing the Assassin to Killian, who caught it in his robotic hand.

Inside the fish tank, Lance couldn't hear what they were saying. He could only watch. And that was enough for him to know that they were the bad guys. "Guess it's time to introduce myself,"

Lance said to a passing clown fish.

He scrolled through the playlists displayed on a gadget attached to his scuba suit until he found "Killer Beatz." Smiling, he pressed Play. Bass started to rumble as the music began until . . .

BOOM!

The fish tank shattered, flooding the room. Lance unzipped the suit to reveal his tux wasn't even wrinkled. He grinned and motioned to the shocked Yakuza to come and get him.

Two Yakuza rushed him, but Lance scooped up two lobsters and attached them to his attackers' faces. Another came at him with a chair, but Lance quickly danced around the guard, who found himself suddenly seated and tied to the chair.

"You know how you can tell when you're the world's greatest spy?" Lance asked, gliding toward Kimura and Killian, smiling.

"Sterling. Lance Sterling," Kimura said with a snarl.

"Everyone knows the name." The smile dropped from Lance's face as he looked to

Killian. "I'm gonna need that case."

Kimura flipped the table with a roar. "Over my dead body!"

Kimura stood. Lance had forgotten how enormous Kimura was. The seven-foot man who could easily beat any sumo wrestler had begun charging at Lance like a bull. Undeterred, Lance casually stepped aside and flipped over the beast of a man, karate-chopping him in the neck.

With a groan, the massive man's eyes rolled back as he was knocked out, and he face-planted into the ground. The remaining Yakuza guards were stunned, some running out of the pagoda into the night.

"Just three ounces of pressure to the vagus nerve in the neck and then look at your boy," Lance explained to the rest of them before turning back to the unconscious Kimura. "Sleepy night night."

Turning back to the main objective of the mission, Lance faced Killian. "That case. Would you mind giving me a 'hand'?" Killian gave him an evil grin, then began to stomp out of the pagoda.

"Oh, hey, come on, what was it—the hand joke?"

Lance shot a tranq dart at Killian, only to watch him catch it with his robotic hand and then promptly toss it aside. Suddenly, Killian whipped around and grabbed Lance by the throat, lifting him into the air. A laser from his left eye scanned Lance's face as Killian began to talk for the first time, in an even, gravelly voice.

"You don't remember me, do you?"

Lance was unnerved by the man's eerily calm demeanor. "What can I say? I meet a lot of bad guys."

The man continued. "I'm going to show you pain like you can't imagine."

Lance squirmed low enough for his feet to touch the ground, where he spotted an eel from the shattered aquarium, flopping around. He kicked it up onto Killian's robotic hand, and the electric eel caused the cybernetics to glitch long enough to release Lance.

Killian threw open the door and ordered the remaining three dozen Yakuza guards into the room.

"Make it hurt," he said plainly as he exited, briefcase in hand.

The Yakuza army surrounded Lance, armed with swords, knives, axes, clubs, and other deadly weapons. Slowly, they began to close in around Lance, who was looking around at them all, hands extended.

"Okay, okay," he said calmly. "You wanna do it the hard way? Let's go, then."

Backed into a corner by the circle of Yakuza, Lance pulled out a lighter. He shook his head in a warning.

"It's about to get messy," Lance said as the Yakuza charged.

Lance pulled the top off of the lighter like a grenade and threw it into the middle of the approaching Yakuza. He braced himself as . . .

PFFT.

A multicolored cloud of glitter filled the air

above the Yakuza, quickly forming into a holo-gram of two kittens playing with each other. The hologram danced through the air, dis-tracting the entire army, most of which had lowered their weapons and were now smiling and "aww"-ing at the sight.

"What the—" Lance was briefly caught up in the moment before shaking his head to clear it, the sound of helicopter blades whirling breaking his attention.

Lance needed a way out, and that way was up. Looking around, he spotted a giant gong nearby. Whipping off his bow tie, he hurled it at the gong's chain, razor edges springing out of the tie and severing the gong from its chain.

The giant BOOOONNNNNGGGG snapped the Yakuza out of their kitten-induced euphoria, and they focused back on Lance, who was now holding the gong like a giant shield, blocking their attacks.

As he reached the middle of the room, he tossed a cuff-link bomb onto the ground under the gong and stood on it. The Yakuza paused, confused.

Lance flashed his trademark grin. "Hey, hey. Don't take the loss so hard. I mean, you did great. And you got to meet Lance Sterling."

FWOOM!

The cuff link exploded on cue and sent Lance through the air like a high-speed elevator. Perfectly timed, Lance soared upward and flipped into Killian's escaping helicopter. He grabbed the Assassin briefcase and leaped out the other side of Killian's aircraft, turning and giving the villain a salute.

Killian merely gave his own ominous smile and turned his helicopter in the opposite direction as Lance rather than pursue the superspy.

"Huh. He gives up easy," Lance said as he pulled a string on his tux, creating wings under the arms that let him glide through the sky, briefcase in hand.

Mission accomplished.

CHAPTER
3

SQUISHY FACE AND
THE EMPTY CASE

It is known that as many as twenty-four million people visit the reflecting pool that stretches between the Lincoln Memorial and the Washington Monument each year. What isn't known is that below the reflecting pool is a super-secret agency of spies working around the clock to keep the nation safe.

The Agency was the sleekest facility in all of Washington, DC, if not the world. Stainless steel blended with touchscreen walls that monitor everywhere in the world. Nothing went unnoticed by the Agency. Even the walls had eyes. And at this moment, all eyes were trained on one person.

Lance Sterling had entered the building.

"He's coming," gasped an elderly security guard, her eyes alight in awe. Other agents applauded.

"Yes, your eyes aren't deceiving you. Yup, it's him. Thank you. Thank you." Lance smiled and waved with one hand, the briefcase in the other.

As he strolled through like a boss, it was clear that everybody wanted to be just like Lance Sterling. To get his approval, or even attention, was everything to the agents. He was a super-star: the best, the brightest, and everyone—including Lance—knew it.

"H-hey, Agent Sterling," called out a pudgy agent, waving. "Looking good!"

Lance waved back. "Hey, not looking so bad yourself, Steve."

"My name is Dave," the agent replied too faintly for Lance to hear.

Two younger male agents Lance had never met before gathered the courage to walk up to him.

"Good morning, sir," said one nervously.

"Fellas! Give it to me." Lance fist-bumped the one who had spoken to him and walked on. Behind him, he could hear the two exchange in excitement.

"Dude, did you see that?" said the fist-bumped agent.

"Never. Wash. That. Hand. Again," the other said, his tone serious.

Lance was at the elevators now and stepped aside to let a trio of gawking agents pass slowly. "Go ahead. All right!" he encouraged.

"Welcome back, Lance," one said.

Lance stepped into the elevator alone. "Thank you. Thank you."

Finally having a moment to himself, he adjusted his tux . . . and glitter puffed out, once more forming a tiny hologram of two kittens playing with a ball of yarn. This time Lance's face darkened.

"Somebody's gonna get it."

The door to the tactical lab where all the spy gadgets were flew open. Techs working on push-broom machine guns, jump-rope laser whips, acid-shooting pens, and other deadly weapons all jumped slightly.

"Oh, Agent Sterling!" The lead tech shifted nervously in her seat.

Lance shook his tux. Kitten glitter once again danced in the air. The techs laughed.

The lead tech knowingly looked at the kitten glitter and said, "Walter Beckett." Everyone pointed to the back of the lab.

Tucked in his corner, almost forgotten, Walter Beckett was attaching a button-sized device to a strange but adorable half-unicorn, half-manatee doll.

"Unitee loves you," it said.

"All right, Unitee," Walter addressed the doll. "Imagine . . . a hydrothermal explosion is about to melt your face off! But what's this? A gadget that can surround you in a pressurized pocket of safety?! Can it work? It hasn't yet, but maybe!" He held a remote. "Okay. Session number nine. Test Thirty-Two."

But Test 32 was interrupted by a loud "AHEM"

from a man in front of his desk. Walter nearly fell backward at the sight.

"Agent Ster—" He cleared his throat. "Agent Sterling?! Uhh, hi. Wow. Umm, Walter Beckett. Pleasure to meet—"

Lance tugged once again on his tux, releasing a cloud of playful kitties. Walter lit up.

"Awww . . . Wait, you used it?! Did it work? Were they—"

"You touched my stuff," Lance said, smiling, staying cool.

Walter grew excited at what this could mean. "Okay, okay, look. I know it's nontraditional but . . ."

Lance put his hand on Walter's shoulder and pushed the young inventor back into his seat. "Feel me here, little man. So, I'm out there, you know, saving the world, doing big things. That's what I do."

Walter nodded in agreement. "Mm-hmm, big things."

"And the way I do it is to have my things do

the things I expect my things to do."

"Yup." Walter gave two thumbs up.

Lance continued. "Like blow stuff up. See, out there, I gotta fight fire with *fire*. Because if I try to fight fire with *glitter* . . ." He leaned in and whispered into Walter's face. ". . . I could get my face get burned off."

Walter excitedly whispered back, oblivious. "But you didn't, because the kitty glitter *worked*."

Lance's head dropped for a moment. Looking back up, he tried a different approach. "Know what works even better? A grenade."

Scrunching his face, Walter looked skeptically at Lance. "It's kinda violent, don't you think?"

Lance began to pace, trying to find a way to get through to the junior genius. "That's the point. You can't save the world with a hug, Wilson."

"It's Walter. And what if you could?!" With that, Walter grabbed his "Unitee" doll and placed a device on the doll's chest before presenting it to Lance. He then pressed a remote and the device deployed an inflatable hug that inflated a giant cushy bubble around Unitee.

"Kind of a personal protection device I've been developing," Walter said confidently. Then silence as the sound of a deflating balloon filled the room and the inflatable hug deflated. Very . . . very . . . slowly. Cocking an eyebrow, Lance shook his head. "That is a vile waste of taxpayer dollars."

"I'm just saying, you can do more by bringing people together than blowing them up. And if I can convince you, *we* can convince the whole Agency."

But Lance was already walking away. "Don't touch my stuff!" he yelled over his shoulder.

"Okay! Okay!" However, an idea struck Walter, who grabbed his backpack and ran to follow Lance out the door. "No, wait, wait, wait!"

He finally caught Lance at the elevator. "Please don't close that door."

Lance pushed the Close Door button rapidly but nothing happened. "Not interested, kid."

"Listen, you gotta hear me out!" Walter said as the doors slowly started to close. He ran for it and got stuck in the sliding doors.

"Whatever it is, no."

The doors squished Walter and his backpack until he was able to squeeze in, and a handful of his gadgets spilled out of his pack, some flying. Lance caught one—a pen that looked like the kind that had buttons to click for different colored ink.

Gathering his gadgets and stuffing them back into his pack, Walter's eyes grew large. This was his chance to pitch his big idea to Lance Sterling, and he didn't intend on blowing it.

"I've been working on this thing at home, right. It's going to change spying forever." He waited for Lance to ask what it was. When the agent didn't, Walter continued anyway. "Imagine if I could make you . . . wait for it . . . drumroll, please . . . DISAPPEEEEEEEAR."

Lance looked at him, disbelieving. "Disappear?"

"Yeah, I'm totally excited about it. It's called biodynamic concealment. Boom! Mic drop."

Pointing to his face, Lance scoffed. "Conceal this? Ha! Nah."

"I mean," Walter went on as Lance toyed with the multi-pen in his hand, "you wouldn't need a bulletproof suit or exploding cuff links. You could blend in everywhere. What if you were totally . . ."

ZAP!

A taser blast shot from the pen and hit Walter, who collapsed to the ground, unable to move a muscle.

". . . invisss-uhh-uhh . . ." Walter couldn't finish his sentence, as his tongue flopped out of his mouth and a pile of drool began to form.

Lance stepped back from the cartoony rubber-hose man that was now Walter Beckett. "Oh! Wow! Dude! That's a mess!"

The muscles in Walter's arm began to regain their ability to move enough to lift his face up as the elevator dinged and the doors opened. "Wait, wait!" Walter shook off the slurring and called to Lance.

"Look, you're the world's greatest spy. Nobody ever listens to my ideas or gives me a chance. But if you did. . . ." Lance bent over and wrapped Walter's fingers around the multi-pen as the young man begged the super-spy. "Together, we could make a difference."

"Make a difference? Boy, I am the difference. All I need from you is when I need a grenade, make me a grenade. Can you do that?" Lance asked seriously.

Walter did his best to shake his head. "There's a better way," he insisted.

Lance looked disappointed. "Wrong answer, Willy. You're fired."

The elevator doors opened and closed, Walter's limp body blocking them. "No, wait! Please don't fire me!"

But it was too late. The Agency's top spy was already gone.

The conference room at the Agency was abuzz as Lance entered. Top agents, techs, and officials were all gathered. In the center of it all was Director Joy Jenkins, standing at the head of a long table.

Lance carefully placed the briefcase on the table next to her.

"Mission accomplished!"

He walked over to the other side of the table, regaling everyone with his harrowing tale of narrow escape as Director Jenkins instructed an agent to carefully begin working to open the case.

"Oh man, I'm telling you, it was one of my best! I was on fire. Fighting, explosions, witty catchphrases."

The agent handed Director Jenkins the case, unlocked and opened. Lance, meanwhile, was pouring himself a cup of coffee.

"Lance." Director Jenkins's voice was terse.

"I had to jump through a flying helicopter!"

"Lance," she repeated, more authority in her voice.

Lance was looking around at everyone, trying to explain how awesome he was on the mission. "It . . . I was . . . Right?!"

"LANCE."

That got his attention. He turned to see Director Jenkins looking incredibly "joyless," her gaze on the case.

"Hm?" he asked, intimidated. The director had never used that tone with him before.

Director Jenkins turned the case to show Lance what was inside. Rather, what *wasn't* inside. Lance's face dropped. The room gasped.

"Please tell me you have an explanation for why this is empty," Director Jenkins said through clenched teeth.

"I know why," said a woman as she entered the room. She was stern, buttoned-up, and all business. That made the smile on her face all the more unnerving, and the words that followed chilling:

"Because he stole it."

CHAPTER
4

TWO LANCE STERLINGS

"**E**xcuse me?!" exclaimed the director and Lance simultaneously at the accusation.

Flashing a badge, the woman announced herself to the room. "Agent Marcy Kappel, Internal Affairs." Everyone shivered. Internal Affairs, or IA, was the most frightening division in the Agency. "Mind if my team sweeps the room?"

"Yes, I mind," replied the director. But her protest went unnoticed as a lanky redheaded girl and a large guy looked like he belonged behind a DJ booth with his massive headphones and baseball cap entered, along with a handful of agents wearing sunglasses even though they were inside.

"They call me Eyes," said the girl in her Scottish accent. "Spectral analysis and quantum optical thermography."

The guy in the baseball cap moved about with his audio satellite, beaming sounds into his headphones. "Ears. Sound."

Eyes and Ears made their way to Lance, who found himself backed into a corner. "Okay, hey, y'all need to ease outta my face right now."

A wave of energy washed over Lance, fired from Ears's audio equipment. Lance suddenly felt as though his suit wasn't high-tech anymore somehow.

"Sonic EMP," explained Ears. "Weapons deactivated. Backin' up."

"Take Agent Sterling into custody." Marcy gave her order, with the confidence of someone who thought they had the hard facts in their pocket.

The IA agents started to advance on Lance before the director put herself between them and her greatest spy.

"All right, enough! We are talking about my

top agent here. I trust this man."

Marcy was unmoved. "The only thing we can trust is the facts." She nodded to the lanky redhead. "Eyes?"

Eyes plugged a cable into the nearest monitor and took control of all the screens in the conference room. "A surveillance camera in Tokyo picked this up two hours after your mission."

The screens lit up and showed Killian's helicopter hovering outside a storage facility. Just then, the Assassin drone exploded out of the aircraft and threw the security guard a dozen feet as though he were a garbage bag. The footage shifted to the pilot and zoomed in on the face.

The pilot was Lance Sterling!

"Lance?" The director's voice was shaken.

The superspy was more surprised than anyone in the room. "Joy—"

He looked around, but no one made eye contact. He'd gone from hero to possible traitor in one video.

Eyes's goggles showed her a readout of

Lance's vitals, including his pulse. "His heart rate just spiked."

Pointing at the screen, Lance yelled, "Because that isn't me!"

"Vocal patterns all off the hook," reported Ears.

Pinching the bridge of her nose and closing her eyes, Joy began pacing. "This has to be wrong. . . ."

Suddenly, Lance remembered something. "This IS wrong. Look, there was a guy with a robot hand there. HE stole the Assassin and scanned my face to frame me!"

"Sure. That sounds plausible and not at all like something you just made up," Marcy scoffed.

Lance's eyes hardened as he walked to Marcy. "You know what? There's a bad guy who needs to be stopped."

"Couldn't agree more," Marcy said as she swiftly bound his wrists in handcuffs.

"Huh," Lance said. "You're good."

Recognizing the tone in his voice when faced with a challenge, Director Jenkins spoke out.

"Lance. Just cooperate."

Unfortunately, Marcy egged on the battle of egos. "Didn't see that coming, did you?" she asked with a smirk.

Lance nodded to his mug. There's a tiny light blinking on it. "Did you see THAT coming?"

Before anyone could react, WHOOOMMMMM, everything went dark as the EMP device knocked out all electronics. In the time it took for the emergency backup generator to kick in, Lance was gone.

"He's running," Marcy sighed. "Why do they always run?"

Lance raced through the streets of Washington, DC, with Marcy and her agents in hot pursuit. He could hear their sirens and see the flashing blue lights around every corner, but there was a reason he was Lance Sterling, Top Spy. He could think three steps ahead of any Internal Affairs agent.

He found a quiet street with a well-hidden overpass into which he quickly pulled his high-tech sports car and took a moment to focus.

"All right, Sterling, think. Think. Somebody else has to know about Robot Hand. But who?"

He let his mind drift back to that night at the pagoda when Robot Hand took the briefcase from . . .

"Kimura!" Lance yelled, then ducked down in case anyone heard him. Straightening up, he pushed a button on the car dash and said, "Find Kimura."

The gentle robotic voice of the car answered, *"Tracking Katsu Kimura."* A holographic head-shot of the beast of a man flickered into view. *Yes!* thought Lance. *Now, let's see where this joker is trying to lie low.* A holo map circled until finally zooming in on a city.

"Playa del Carmen, Mexico," Lance said, just as a siren blipped out an alert near him.

Lance felt the agents closing in. They couldn't take him, not now that he had a lead on clearing his name! He needed to run. *No,* he thought.

"I need to disappear. . . ."

CHAPTER
5

THE FUTURE OF ESPIONAGE

Walter lived in a house on a quiet row of average-looking houses in the quiet suburb of Alexandria, just outside of DC. It wouldn't take a superspy to figure out which house belonged to him: His was the only one with a giant pigeon coop on top.

Walter entered his home, dejected and carrying a box of his belongings in his arms. The house was organized chaos, with parts and devices taken apart in various stages and other inventions ready to be tried. He walked past a row of pictures that hung in the hallway. A few were of Walter and his mom. His favorite was of young Walter, standing next to his mom in her

uniform—and wearing Walter's wrist gadget!—
surrounded by her fellow officers after she won
an award. The last one was a shadow box of his
mom in her uniform, a folded flag, and her police
badge. Walter glanced at it as he dropped the
box on the ground in his work area. *I could really
use your company today, Mom*, he thought.

"Unitee . . ." came the muffled voice of the
Unitee doll, but Walter ignored it. Instead he
turned on the TV, and Korean voices came from
the screen. *Hearts in Seoul*, a popular Korean
soap opera, was playing. Walter perked up
slightly as two lovers were reunited.

"Cooo," announced a cute brown-and-white
pigeon as she landed on his shoulder.

Walter sighed, still watching the screen as
he shared a snack with her. "See, Lovey? Some
dreams do come true."

DING!

The sound of a timer cut through the air.
Walter looked over; it was from his 3-D molecu-
lar printer. Instantly, a thousand thoughts began

to race through his mind. This was it. What he'd been working on. Would it work? Oh gosh. "Oh. Ummm, uhhh. Okay." He needed to breathe.

He gathered his thoughts and pushed a small button on the side of the printer. The machine sprung to life in a series of whirls, clicks, and beeps until finally it produced a small vial full of a glowing blue serum.

Walter hit Record on his laptop's camera and began to speak out loud. "Commencing bio-dynamic concealment test number eighty-three, batch five." He motioned to Lovey, who flew to his side. "Umm, Lovey, could I borrow a feather, please?"

Lovey ruffled her feathers, and a soft feather floated down into Walter's hand.

"Thank you. Here's a little something for you," he said, giving Lovey a handful of birdseed. He then placed the feather into an empty beaker.

He picked up the vial of blue serum and braced himself. "If this works, they'll have to give me my old job back."

He carefully poured a few drops of the serum into the beaker holding the feather. For a second, nothing happened, until . . . the blue serum became clear and began to bubble as the chemical reaction took place. Walter's jaw hit the floor.

"No. Way . . . It worked? It *worked*." He started to do a victory dance, holding the beaker in his hand. "It worked! It worked! Lovey, it worked! It—"

"I need to disappear."

Agent Lance Sterling was standing in his living room. Looking VERY serious and watching Walter dance.

Walter freaked out. "Ahhhh!!! Whoa!!! Wha— How did you . . . ? What are you doing in my, errr . . ." Walter cleared his throat and tried to act casual. "What's up?"

Walter watched as Lance looked around and tried not to touch anything. Maybe he was afraid glitter kittens might be hidden somewhere. "Okay, listen, that next-generation concealment tech you were talking about earlier . . . say I believed you. You wouldn't happen to have it on hand, would you?

"Actually, I happen to have it IN hand," Walter answered, nodding to the beaker, but Lance wasn't paying attention.

"Show it to me."

Walter didn't get, well, ANY visitors, so he was unsure how to act, especially around the spy who had him fired who happened to now be in his house asking for Walter's help. A nice beverage always seemed to work on TV.

"Sure! Umm, first, well, can I offer you a drink? I've got water, Soylent drinkable meal replacement—"

Lance impatiently grabbed the beaker out of Walter's hand and drank the formula in one gulp.

"Mmmm. Good. We had a drink. So, what kinda tech are we talking? Light-bending camo suit? Adaptive response—Blech!" Lance shuddered. "Was that diet? Has a weird aftertaste. Anyway, where's the tech?"

Walter was in such shock that he had barely

heard a word Lance had said. He pointed at the beaker in Lance's hand, then at Lance's mouth. "Umm, well, y-y-you just drank it."

"Drank what?"

"The tech," answered Walter. "Now it's gone. Yup."

Walter had begun to pace, trying to figure out a way to tell the world's greatest spy what was about to happen to him. It struck him to use visual aids. He activated a projector beam on his watch that showed a strand of DNA changing.

Before Walter could open his mouth, Lance held up his hand. "Wow! That's cool, and I'm sure you have some science mumbo-jumbo speech that goes with it, but here's what I need you to do. Pretend like you're a normal person talking to a much-cooler normal person."

"In precisely forty-five seconds, you will transform into a pigeon." Walter folded his arms and smiled nervously.

Lance stared at Walter. And stared more. He kept staring, as if he was waiting for the punch line. When Lance realized the tech specialist he had fired earlier that day was serious, he shook his head.

"I'm out," Lance said, drawing the line at pigeons. He turned to leave, followed by Walter.

"Wait, wait, wait! What you're about to experience is the future of espionage!" Walter insisted.

"Ok—urggle." A wave of nausea washed over Lance, causing him to double over in pain.

Walter pointed, as though he were narrating *Planet Earth*. "You might be experiencing some mild discomfort."

"AAAGGGHHHHH!!!"

"Or severe. I'll make note of that," Walter continued scientifically.

Lance began stumbling about the house, trying to find the front door. "This is because I fired you, right? Now I'm gonna walk outta here."

"Yeah, that might be hard."

Lance propped himself up on the kitchen table and wheezed, "Okay, I might pass out."

Walter's eyes were bright as he watched his life's achievement happening before him. "Oh, you're definitely going to pass out. Aaaand there you go," Walter said as Lance fell to the ground. Walter continued his explanation. "Your genomes are being smashed apart so they can be reassembled with pigeon DNA."

"What did you do to me? You poisoned me," Lance insisted.

Eyeing a clock on the wall, Walter dismissed the accusation. "I wouldn't do that." His voice began to shake with nervous excitement. "Three seconds . . ."

"Three seconds?!" Lance asked incredulously.

"You're going to be fine. Trust me," Walter said, unable to hide his excitement. "Here we go!"

In a flash, Lance disappeared, his tuxedo falling to the ground.

Walter rushed to him. "Lance? Lance." He spotted where Lance had been and uttered in amazement, "It worked."

He reached out to grab Lance. "Subject's vitals appear stable. Inserting rectal thermometer."

That was enough for Lance. No way was he getting a rectal thermometer. He swatted at Walter's hands, but to his utter horror he didn't have an arm. He had swatted with a wing! Glancing around at himself, it dawned on him what Walter's serum had made him.

Lance Sterling, superspy, was now a PIGEON!

CHAPTER
6

UN-BIRD ME

"AHHHHHHHHHHHHHHHHHHHHHH!!!!!"

Lance was freaking out. REALLY freaking out. The kind of freaking out you do when you turn into a pigeon. Instead of arms, he had two tiny wings. Instead of legs, he had two skinny bird legs with tiny bird feet attached to them. And instead of skin, he was covered from beak to butt in bright blue feathers. He also had dark feathers on his belly and at the bottom of his neck, which formed a marking that looked remarkably like a bow tie. Not exactly appreciating this new look, Lance continued to scream.

"It's okay, buddy," Walter said. "Hey, it's okay.

Don't you worry. Your good friend Walter is here." Walter still seemed focused on the fact that his invention actually worked rather than the fact that he just turned the world's greatest spy into a bird.

But Lance didn't hear Walter over his internal and external screams. Lance stumbled across the kitchen floor like he had just gotten off some horrible roller-coaster ride and was ready to hurl in the nearest trash can.

"Subject appears disoriented," Walter said, observing Lance's behavior.

"Of course I'm disoriented!" Lance squawked.

"You can talk!" Walter said. He turned to Lovey, who was watching the scene unfold with a casual curiosity. "Lovey, he can talk!"

Lovey didn't reply to this because she, unlike Lance, couldn't talk. But Walter didn't mind. He was still in disbelief. "It worked! It worked! Can you believe this?"

"My eyes!" Lance shouted. "What did you do to my eyes?!"

Walter was beaming with excitement. "Hey, Lance, look at me!"

"Look at you?!" Lance shouted. "I can't NOT look at you, Walter. I can see *my butt* and *your face* at the *same time*."

Lance tried to focus his eyes. Instead of seeing just Walter, Lance saw Walter, Lovey, everything to his left, everything to his right, and his downy butt all at the same time! The feeling could only be described as a swirling psychedelic kaleidoscope of . . . weird.

"That is so cool!" Walter said, not reading the room. "Fact: Pigeons have three-hundred-and-sixty-degree vision. Now nobody can sneak up behind you!"

As if Lance wasn't already fuming, Lovey teetered over and sweetly nuzzled him. Lance jumped at this invasion of his now-much-smaller personal space.

"Stop, girl!" Lance said. "Come on!"

Unfazed, Walter continued to ramble off pigeon facts. "This is so great! Pigeons can be found in every major city around the world and no one notices them. It's the most perfect form a spy can take."

Lovey, who was still pressing up against Lance's feathers, received a rather awkward pigeon foot to the face. She didn't seem to mind because this foot belonged to Lance. And she REALLY liked Lance. Lance, on the other hand, had other things on his mind.

Lance whipped toward Walter, his big bird eyebrows pointed in anger.

"You better UN-BIRD me. Right. Now!" he demanded. "That's it! I'M NOT PLAYING WITH YOU! UN-BIRD—"

Lance stopped himself and took a deep breath. "I'm raising my voice. I probably shouldn't be raising my voice at you. I guess you could imagine, I'm a little stressed right now. I need you to un-bird me, Walter."

"Mm-hmm. Of course," Walter replied. "I'll start working on an antidote right now."

"START?!" Lance snapped.

"Well, the formula was purely theoretical until—"

"You're going to 'start'?" Lance asked. "YOU DON'T HAVE AN ANTIDOTE?"

Lovey seemed to like this side of Lance, because she began to nuzzle him again.

"Stop, girl. Seriously!" Lance muttered out of the side of his beak. He pushed her off again, hoping she would take the hint this time. "Okay. Okay. So you birded me. And you can't un-bird me."

"Technically you kinda birded yourself," Walter replied.

Lance gave an exasperated laugh. "Oh, I'm gonna hurt this boy. I'm gonna hurt the boy."

"No, no, look, I know you're upset, but everything's okay," Walter assured Lance. "I called the Agency and told them you were here."

"You did *what*?!" Lance shouted.

"No, no, no, it's okay," Walter explained. "I didn't tell them that you're a bird. Although I think they'll figure that out pretty quickly."

53

"I gotta ghost!" Lance said, teetering off on his new bird legs.

BOOM!

Lance had slammed headfirst into a glass door. Walter and Lovey cringed.

"Yeah. There may be one or two downsides to your new form," Walter said.

Lance took a deep breath, but his words still came out dripping with anger. "Webster. Open. The. Door." Lance's eyes told Walter that he meant it.

"Okay. Okay," Walter said. He reluctantly opened the door and Lance strode through.

CHAPTER
7

GOD OF THE ASPHALT

Walter followed Lance out the door. Still not totally in control of his new bird body, Lance tumbled down the front steps of Walter's house. The guilt of turning the Agency's greatest agent into a bird was beginning to sink in for Walter. At the same time, he was confused about why Lance didn't want the Agency's help. The Agency was Lance's whole life! At least that's what it seemed like from the outside.

Walter tried to stop Lance from face-planting against the sidewalk at the bottom of the stairs. "Why are you running from the Agency?"

"Get off me!" Lance replied, swatting Walter away with his wing. He then got up and stumbled down the driveway. Beyond frustrated with everything that had happened to him in the last few hours, he turned toward Walter. "I'm running because there's a bad guy out there with my face, and now I have to try to stop him from hurting people while being a BIRD. And thank you for that! Thank you very much for that! You know what, you're fired! Double fired!"

Walter squinted. "I don't think that's a thing."

"Oh, it's a thing!" Lance shot back. "It's a thing now!"

Lance angrily waddled off, as angrily as one can waddle. Walter watched him go, not exactly sure what to do. Lance waddled to his car but was a bit taken aback by its size. Was it always this big? Suddenly, Lance saw that the driver's side window was open just a crack. That was his way in.

"Okay," Lance said to himself, spreading his wings. "It's a wingsuit. How hard could it be?" Lance took a second to muster up a bit more of his signature Lance Sterling confidence. "Time to fly."

Lance attempted to fly but ended up smacking right into the car door, beakfirst. He flopped pathetically on the ground. Lance thought for a minute. If he could get to the roof of the car, then he could slip in through the slightly opened sunroof. With his new plan in place, Lance shimmied up the tire and onto the hood of the car.

"You broke into the Kremlin using a napkin and a piece of duct tape," he reminded himself. On the hood, Lance took a flying leap onto the windshield. He then used his tiny body to power himself up, trying to reach the roof.

"You should . . . be able . . . to get . . . into your own . . . car!"

SQUEEEEEEEEEEEK.

Lance slid down the windshield. But don't you know, you can't keep a good spy down. He tried again. Lance climbed all the way to the top of the windshield. . . .

SQUEEEEEEEEEEEEEEEEEEEK.

He slid all the way back down. Again. But he gave it another try. This time, he gave it his all.

SQUEEEEEEEEEEEEEEEEEEEEEEEEEEEEEEEEEEK.

"Oh, COME ON!" Lance shouted. He sat on the hood of car, out of breath and out of any hope that he was going to get himself into his car. Lance glanced up to see Walter standing there, holding his backpack and a little out of breath. He must have run inside to get the backpack when Lance was distracted.

"Okay, wait, hear me out—"

"Is someone talking?" Lance asked sarcastically, refusing to look at Walter. "I don't hear anybody talking. Especially somebody that's been double-fired, working on a triple fire."

"I'll come with you!" Walter said. "I can show you all the advantages of being a pigeon and how it can make you an even better spy, and then you'll give me my job back! We both win!"

"All right, let me think about that," Lance replied. Walter's eyes grew hopeful. "No."

Lance turned to hear sirens blare in the distance. He looked back at Walter, who had his arms folded defiantly.

"Okay, I suppose you have somebody else who has a mobile lab and can turn you back into a man . . ." Walter said, letting his voice trail off.

Lance stared at Walter. How could this kid be the only thing standing between Lance and being human again?

Lance banged his tiny head against the car in frustration. "Errghhhh! Get in the car!"

Walter popped into the passenger seat. "You won't even know I'm here."

The sirens grew louder and louder until they saw Marcy's SUV race up the street. Walter looked at the empty driver's seat, then out through the windshield.

Lance was still sitting on the hood, with a deadpan look on his face. "I'll just ride out here. Don't worry."

"Oh, right. My bad." Walter jumped out of the car and ran to open the driver's side door just as the ominous black SUV screeched to halt behind them.

Marcy's voice boomed over the scratchy loudspeaker. "Agent Lance Sterling! Exit the premises NOW or we will use extreme force!"

Walter stared at the SUV as if he were a

deer in headlights. Suddenly, an entire SWAT team advanced toward Walter's house as helicopters appeared overhead. Bright spotlights circled the house every which way.

"What are you doing? Get in the car!" Lance shouted. "Wilfred! Let's go!"

Walter did as he was told and ran back around to the passenger side. "They're destroying my house!" he said, hopping back in the car.

Walter buckled himself in as Lance hopped up on the steering wheel. It looked as if Lance was going to drive.

"Activate auto-drive," Lance commanded the car computer.

"Auto-drive engaged," it responded as the steering wheel disappeared into the console.

Lance smirked. He knew exactly where he wanted to go. "Sterling private jet hangar."

He turned confidently toward Walter. "See that. You can bird me, but you can't stop me— OMMPH!" Just then, the car peeled out, throwing little Lance back against the seat.

Meanwhile in Marcy's SUV, she sighed as she watched Lance's car race off down the street. *You gotta be kidding me*, she thought. Marcy had just realized that Lance was definitely not in Walter's house because he had been parked behind them the entire time.

Marcy floored it. "Eyes, Ears, buckle up. And get me everything we have on that Beckett kid."

"You think they're working together?" Eyes asked.

Marcy shook her head. "Sterling works alone. He's using him for something."

SKREEEEEECH.

Lance's car took a hard right. Walter was holding on for dear life, when Lovey popped out of his backpack.

"You brought the lady bird??" Lance asked, exasperated.

"She's my emotional support animal," Walter replied.

"You're going to need a *life* support animal if that bird poops in my ca—" Before Lance could finish, he caught sight of Marcy's SUV in the rearview mirror. She was pulling up fast.

"Ugh," Lance said. "We got company."

Marcy weaved around the other pursuing SUVs the Agency had sent. She was quickly closing the gap between her and Lance's car. If someone was going to catch Lance, it was going to be her. Marcy led the chase, while her team gave her updates on the pursuit.

"We've got units blocking every street, over-pass, and exit within a five-mile radius," Eyes reported, zooming in with her specialized glasses.

Marcy smiled. "Perfect. Time for a cattle drive."

"Saddle up!" Ears shouted.

Marcy's entire fleet of SUVs knew this plan well. Two SUVs ominously sped up in order to move in front of Lance's car. Suddenly, they skidded to a halt, cutting the superspy off at the pass.

Just as Lance's car was about to slam straight into the SUVs, Lance, Walter, and Lovey heard the car computer calmly announce: *"Evasive maneuvers activated."*

The spy car spun in an impossible maneuver and . . .

SPLAT!

They missed the SUVs by the narrowest of margins but . . .

SPLAT!

Every time the cars turned . . .

SPLAT!

SPLAT!

SPLAT!

SPLAT!

. . . Lance splatted against the window.

"I don't have time for this!" Lance spat out between splats. "Activate weapons!"

"WHAT?!" Walter shouted.

But the car computer did what it was told.

"Activating weapons."

"Relax," Lance told Walter. "I'm just gonna take out her tires."

"Deactivating weapons."

Wait, what?

Walter had deactivated the weapons by pressing the Disengage button on the display panel.

"No. No. We're the good guys! We can't shoot the other good guys!" Walter said.

"You're right, Walter," Lance replied sarcastically. "Let's just pull over and talk it out."

Walter was so relieved "Exactly! Can we?"

"Activate weapons!" Lance shouted, ignoring Walter's question.

"Activating weapons."

"Deactivate weapons!" Walter said.

"Deactivating weapons."

Walter knew he needed to come up with a better solution. He quickly scrolled through the gadgets on the car's computer.

"How about something nonlethal?" Walter suggested. "Like, ummmm . . . oil slick."

"Activate weapons!" Lance shouted at the car.

"Deactivate weapons!" Walter also shouted at the car.

"Activate weapons!"

"Oil slick!"

"Activate weapons!"

"Oil slick!"

"Weapons!"

"Oil slick!"

Marcy, Eyes, and Ears watched as weapons popped in and out of Lance's car.

In and out.

In and out.

In and out.

Ears broke the confused silence. "This man is trippin'."

Meanwhile, back in the spy car, the back-and-forth button-pushing had escalated into an all-out slap fight.

After Walter landed a few good slaps, Lance ended the fight with a peck to Walter's hand with his sharp beak. Walter yelped in pain and pulled his hand away.

"HA!" Lance cried, victorious.

"System shutdown. Goodbye." With that, the steering wheel reappeared, sliding into place on

the car's console.

Lance started to panic. "What did you do?!"

With no one to steer it, the car lurched wildly and jumped onto the sidewalk. Lance flew onto the steering wheel, desperate to regain control. The car turned and headed straight toward a tractor trailer!

"AHHHHHHHHHHH!!!" Lance and Walter screamed in unison. The car spun, sliding under the trailer—and miraculously reappearing on the other side unscathed.

The trailer cut off Marcy's pursuit. The agents' SUV screeched to a halt.

"He's like a god of the asphalt," Ears said.

Marcy's eyes narrowed. "We'll see about that."

She pulled into oncoming traffic, expertly weaving in and out between the cars. Like it was no effort at all, Marcy hopped the median and was back on Lance's tail.

The spy car swerved dangerously along the road as Lance began to run back and forth on the steering wheel. Against all odds, this was actually working. A pigeon was *officially* driving a car!

But Walter couldn't find the excitement in this scientific breakthrough because he was in the middle of a nervous breakdown. "Oh no!! No!! Oh no!!" he shouted.

"I got this. I got this. I got this," Lance chanted.

Suddenly, Walter saw that they were coming up on a major intersection. They were toast.

"We're gonna die!" Walter announced.

"Oh, no we're not," Lance said, eyes locked dead ahead.

The superspy jumped on the other end of the steering wheel and cranked it hard. The car, along with Walter and the two pigeons, careened through the intersection and down several flights of steps.

"AHHHHHHHHHHHHH!!!"

Marcy and team raced down the street in hot pursuit. "We should be coming up on him any second," she said.

BOOM!

Lance's car sailed overhead and landed hard, right in front of them.

"What the—" Eyes began to ask.

But before she could finish, they saw Walter—and two pigeons—bouncing around the inside of the car. When Walter knocked the gearshift into reverse, Marcy, Eyes, and Ears watched as Lance's car rocketed down the road driving backward!

Marcy had had enough. "This ends now." She picked up her communicator. "Is everyone in position?"

"Affirmative," the agent on the other end responded.

Marcy's team had set up a roadblock on the other side of the overpass under construction.

There was nowhere left for Lance to go.

Like Marcy, Lance also had had enough.

"Walter! Get that computer back online!" Lance commanded.

"Systems coming back online . . ." Walter

said as he worked to get the computer humming to life again.

"Defensive applications online."

The computer screen lit up with an array of buttons, each displaying a different gadget from smoke screen to ejector seat.

"Oil slick??" Walter asked again.

"Fine! Whatever! Just press it—WAIT!" Lance said, realizing something, "We're driving backward!"

But it was too late. Oil spurted out of the back of the car, right under its own tires. The car spun out at full speed. Lance's car scraped along the guardrail, sparks igniting the oil slick. . . .

FOOSH!

Marcy's SUV skidded to a halt. She found herself surrounded by a ring of fire from the ignited oil slick! The entire team watched in utter amazement as Lance's car spun off an overpass and casually landed on the top of a car carrier cruising down the highway below.

"That was tight," Ears said.

"Yup, its official. I'm a fan," Eyes added.

Marcy squinted into the distance as the car carrier drove out of sight. "Did anyone else see a pigeon in that car?"

"Auto-drive engaged."

A petrified Lance hung on Walter's face.

"I can't help but feel like some of this is my fault—" Walter began.

"Some?!" Lance shouted, incredulous. "JOKER, this is ALL YOUR FAULT!" He turned to the car computer.

"Airstrip. Now!"

CHAPTER
8

FLYING HIGH

Somewhere between Washington, DC, and Mexico, a supercool stealth spy plane streaked through the sky.

They had arrived at the airstrip and boarded Lance Sterling's private jet. Using the intel he had gathered on Kimura before turning into a pigeon, Lance set a course for the Mayan Riviera Resort in Mexico. Inside the main cabin of the plane, Walter and Lovey were safely tucked into their seats with seat belts fastened.

Walter riffled through his backpack excitedly. "Lovey, this is the opportunity we've been waiting for!" he said. "There are so many gadgets I want to test in the field. We got the binder bubbles, collide-oscope, hypno-stars, blamethrower, snore-pedo! We've got the multi-pen! We haven't even tried the multi-pen in the . . ."

Walter gasped, realizing. "I'm gonna need a code name."

His voice took on a very bad British accent. "Bond . . . Hydrogen Bond."

Walter attempted to debonairly sip from his juice box, as debonairly as one could sip from a juice box.

This was quickly interrupted when Walter began to hear Lance shouting from behind the closed bathroom door. "Oh! Oh no! Where is it?" Lance yelled.

"Wait?! What is that?!" Lance continued. "WHAT IS THAT?!"

The jet jumped through the air, hitting some turbulence.

"No," Lance said to himself. "Fly, fly, fly, fly, flyyyyyyyyy!"

Walter and Lovey winced as they heard a cacophony of horrifying sounds coming from the bathroom. There was flapping, scrapping, thumping, and then finally the familiar whir of the hand dryer. This was followed by a long horrified scream, then a splash, flush, and the sounds of a pigeon struggling to climb out of a toilet. And finally, the bathroom door swung open and Lance stomped out, soaking wet and dragging toilet paper behind him.

"Heeeey, everything go okay in there?" Walter asked, knowing the answer.

"I just found out that number one and number two both come out the same place," Lance replied. "So no, things are not okay."

Lance furiously struggled to get the toilet paper off his foot.

"Yeah, it's called a cloaca," Walter explained, trying to be helpful. "It's sounds weird and gross. But having a cloaca just means—"

"DUDE! I know what it means. I saw it in the mirror," Lance said. He climbed into his chair and took out his tablet, indicating that he was finished talking about his cloaca. Lance pulled up

Kimura's mug shot and map of Mexico.

"I know you're not in a good place right now, but there are benefits to being a pigeon," Walter said.

Lance snapped. "Okay, so read what used to be my lips: You are only here because (a) I can't work a touch screen enough to eject you, and (b) you were supposed to be working on something, correct?"

"Oh, the antidote. Right. Sure," Walter said. He typed on the screen next to him until it displayed what looked like a very complicated DNA program.

"Yeah, that's going to take eighteen hours to render," Walter said.

"I'm stuck like this with this body for eigh—" Lance stopped himself, stamping around in a circle on his chair. If he wasn't such an angry pigeon, it would actually be kind of cute.

"Oooooooh, hoooo boy! Woooo. Okay, walk this one off," Lance said, trying to calm himself down.

He stopped and refocused on his tablet's screen. Lance gestured with his wing toward Kimura's mugshot, the map of Mexico, and the security footage of Killian wearing his face. "How am I gonna make him tell me where the guy with the robotic hand is?" Lance asked Walter. "Peck at him?!"

"You know, being a pigeon is actually way cooler than it seems," Walter tried again. "And if you just embrace your new form, you'll see all the advantages."

Lovey fluttered next to Lance as Walter went on. "Like, fact: Did you know that pigeons can see in slow motion? Because, fact: Pigeons can fly up to ninety-two point seven miles per hour. And, fact: Pigeons are highly intelligent animals who like to play games. Oh, and FACT—"

"FACT: You shoulda kept your seat belt on!" Lance interrupted.

Suddenly, he hit a giant eject button. Walter was sucked right out of the plane all while Lance laughed maniacally.

Not really.

This is what Lance wished would've happened. Instead, he continued to sit there listening to Walter rattle off pigeon facts while Lovey snuggled up against him.

"Fact: Pigeons can see ultraviolet light, which is a broad spectrum of light the human eye can't even see . . ." Walter continued.

Lance was officially doomed to endure Walter's litany of facts as the stealth spy plane streaked toward the horizon.

"Fact: Pigeons have excellent homing abilities. And, fact . . ."

CHAPTER
9

WINGMAN

PLAYA DEL CARMEN, MEXICO

Lance, Walter, and Lovey arrived to a gorgeous open-air luxury hotel bustling with tourists. It just so happened that Lance and Lovey weren't the only pigeons at this hotel. The open roof made it so that pigeons were flying in and out and roosting in the palm trees.

"All right, Kimura," Lance said. "I'm coming for you. Lance Sterling is on the scene."

Back in his terrible British accent, Walter announced himself as well. "And Bond. Hydrogen Bond."

"Dude. You need medicine," Lance said. He quickly refocused on the mission at hand, taking note of a flock of pigeons gathering in an adjacent courtyard as well as a half dozen of Kimura's armed Yakuza patrolling the hotel entrance. Lance nodded and gestured with his wings. Oh. It's ON.

"These fools," Lance said. "All right, y'all better squad up, 'cause here comes the—"

Walter quickly pushed Lance back with his foot.

"Hey!" Lance shouted. "Did you just toe-poke me?"

"You're a pigeon," Walter replied out of the corner of his mouth, not wanting it to look like he was talking to a pigeon. "You can walk right past them."

Realizing that Walter was correct, Lance lowered his wings and hesitantly waddled on. Just in case, he continued to keep one of his eyes on the Yakuza as he passed.

"Just a regular old bird," Lance assured no one in particular. "Caw!"

"Uh, that's not a pigeon sound," Walter

whispered as he casually walked behind Lance.

"Until you grow a cloaca, I decide what the bird sounds are," Lance snapped back.

Lance continued to make crazy birds sounds as he waddled, with Walter following. He couldn't believe this was actually working.

Lance laughed. "It's so stupid."

One of the Yakuza gave Lance a weird look . . . but then shrugged, completely dismissing it.

"You see," Walter said to Lance, "it's like you're invisible."

Lance, Walter, and Lovey finally made it inside the lobby. Lance then climbed up on the lobby couch to get a better view. From there he spotted the receptionist desk. Lance observed the receptionist helping a new guest check in. She smiled as she handed him his room key.

"Bingo," Lance said.

Walter leaned in close to Lance's face. "Okay, let's figure this out. You and me. Let's go. Let's brainstorm. How we gonna find this nut?"

"Uhh, you are going to sit down right here on

this very nice couch," Lance replied.

"But I'm you're wingman," Walter said.

"Oooh, you know who needs a wingman?" Lance asked sarcastically. "That couch. Go sit your narrow behind down and do some science stuff. And I'm gonna go find Kimura. Alone."

Lance took a step toward the front desk, but suddenly he smelled something. . . .

"Oh, what is that heavenly smell?" Lance asked. "Mnunm."

Lance looked up to see what he was actually smelling was a gross piece of bread on the floor.

"Oh no. Do not do it, Lance," he pleaded with himself as he leaned in for a bite. "Ugh. Lance! Have some dignity."

But Lance couldn't stop himself and began to eat the bread like a common bird!

"Walter! What is happening?" Lance asked between mouthfuls.

Walter tapped on his watch, recording this peculiar observation before answering. "Uhh, must be some sort of latent avian instincts kicking in."

"Why am I eating food off the ground?! Why does it taste amazing?!" Lance continued to ask.

Just then, two pigeons fluttered over to join in on the food. Breaking their focus from the deliciously gross bread, they watched Lance curiously. They'd never met a talking bird before! Lance barely noticed them as he continued to gorge on the floor food next to an overflowing garbage can. He slurped up an old noodle, only to discover Lovey was on the other end!

"Eww. Nah. I'm good. Thank you," Lance said to Lovey. He was not about to be a part of some warped *Lady and the Tramp* moment with Walter's pet pigeon. No way.

One of the pigeons, a gangly old bird with a skinny neck, coughed up an old Band-Aid. He offered this to Lance.

"OH, wow," Lance said, backing away. But the larger pigeon, with a big fluffy belly, crowded Lance back toward the group.

"My dude," Lance said, addressing the large pigeon, "Seriously. Gimme ten feet."

None of the other pigeons seemed to

understand this, because they only just crowded in closer.

"No. Human feet. Back up," Lance said.

Unfazed, the scrawny Band-Aid–wielding pigeon slurped his offering back up.

Lance tried to contain his repulsion. "OH! Nah. I wish I could unsee that."

Meanwhile, Walter observed these interactions. His eyes grew wide with excitement.

"This is huge," he said to Lance. "They've made you part of their flock!"

"I'm not trying to be part of nobody's flock." Lance replied. He gestured with his wings toward the pigeons. "Shoo! Back up, fanboy."

"Coo! Coo!" the large pigeon replied.

"I don't care that your name is Jeff!" Lance said in response. "Beat it!"

"You can understand them?!" Walter said, amazed.

Lance's eyes went wide, horrified. "WHAT?! No. No! Not hearing bird talk!"

"Does Lovey really love me?" Walter asked.

"Am I her best friend?" Walter followed a ruffled Lance as he pushed through the pigeons. "Nice to meet you, Jeff!" Walter called out.

"Stop talking to Jeff!" Lance shouted at Walter behind him. Lance stomped toward the receptionist desk, not noticing that Jeff and the other scrawny bird had also followed.

Lance had a plan. When the receptionist walked away to take a phone call, Lance climbed up onto the counter. He quickly pecked Kimura's name into the hotel's computer.

Nothing.

"All right, what alias are you using, Kimura?" Lance asked himself.

He pecked at the keys, and the room charges began to scroll up. He tapped the room number at the top, and Kimura's face popped up.

"Notkimura," Lance said. "Wow. That's clever."

He pecked at the keys again and managed to print out a brand-new room key for Kimura's room. Completely undetected.

"I am way too good at this," Lance remarked.

Just as Lance was about to grab the key card, Jeff and the scrawny pigeon landed on the desk.

"Oh, come on. Seriously, fellas," Lance said. "Not now."

Lance struggled to pick up the key card with his wings and beak. It continued to slide back and forth along the counter. Pathetic.

"This is so humiliating," Lance whined.

DING!

Lance whirled around to see the scrawny old bird pecking at the hotel bell.

"Hey!" Lance yell-whispered. "I'm not for the games!"

Jeff, who was innocently standing next to the scrawny bird, leaned down. He was about to ring the bell.

"You better—NO! Nuh-uh," Lance said.

But Jeff just leaned closer . . .

"Stop it!" Lance said.

. . . and closer . . .

"Stop it! STOP!" Lance pleaded.

Jeff paused. Then . . .

DING!

DING!

Jeff pecked the bell.

"NO!" Lance shouted as the scrawny bird joined in.

DING!

DING!

DING!

"Stop it!" Lance said. "What is wrong with you?"

All of a sudden Jeff and the scrawny bird flew off. Lance turned back for the key card only to find the receptionist staring down at him menacingly. *Oh*, Lance thought. Now he understood why they flew away.

WHAM!

The receptionist smacked Lance with her giant keyboard and swiped him into a garbage bag.

"Ratas con alas . . ." she muttered, tossing the bag out into the alley. She obviously had something against pigeons to think of them as rats with wings.

Lance dug himself out of the trash bag and fell

to the ground, dazed and hurt. When he looked up, he saw Jeff and the scrawny bird staring down at him. Lance noticed that it looked like the scrawny one had something wide lodged in its throat. Right after this thought crossed Lance's mind, the bird retched and coughed up . . . the room key card! It landed unceremoniously, wet and nasty, on Lance's face.

Moments later, Lance stormed past Walter. Jeff and his scrawny friend were right behind him.

"Well, would you look at that," Walter said. "Being in a flock helped you."

"Not my flock!" Lance shot back. He teetered over to the elevator, Walter close behind him.

"Wait, wait, wait, wait!" Walter shouted after him. "You should not go up there alone. Maybe I have something else that can help—" Walter reached for his backpack.

"Walter!" Lance said. "I. Do. Not. Need. Your. *Help.* Never will."

With that, the elevator doors closed in Walter's face. Then they automatically opened again. Lance looked at Walter, deadpan.

"Can you push twenty for me, please?" he asked.

Walter leaned into the elevator, pressed the button for the twentieth floor, and leaned back out of the elevator.

"I thought you didn't need any help," Walter said.

"I don't," Lance replied.

"Feels like helping," Walter said, the doors closing again.

"Nope," Lance said. The doors were now completely closed.

"Yeah, a little bit," Walter said to himself.

"Didn't," Lance responded from behind the elevator doors. It started to ascend.

"Did," Walter said.

"Did NOT!"

CHAPTER
10
ROOM SERVICE

Kimura was in a state of bliss, floating in his luxury hotel room's indoor pool. He was definitely in need of some rest and relaxation. Thanks to Lance Sterling, he was in a neck brace with a broken nose and two black eyes.

But Kimura wasn't dumb. He still had security cameras watching every corner of his room and hallway, just in case.

But a small pigeon outside his room with a key card was hard to spot on grainy security footage.

Just then, Kimura heard the sound of his hotel room door shutting. Then the blinds began to shut one by one.

"Who's there?!" Kimura called out. He climbed

out of the pool and wrapped a towel around him-self. "Talk! While you still have lips."

Lance's voice boomed from inside the dark room. "Shut it, Kimura."

"Sterling?!" Kimura said, shocked. He franti-cally searched for his weapons on a side table. He was about to lunge for a sword when—

"Nuh-uh," Lance's voice said. "Eyes front! Hands up!"

Kimura put his hands up, which also allowed his towel to drop to the floor.

"Oooh. Scratch that," Lance said. "Pick up your towel. One hand up."

"What do you want?!" Kimura demanded.

"Here's how this works: I ask the questions. You answer," Lance said.

Little did Kimura know, Lance the pigeon was on the floor behind him. Lance began to speak again, but he turned to see Lovey, Jeff, and the scrawny third bird with no name land next to him.

"What?!" Lance said to the apparently magi-cal pigeons next to him.

"What?" Kimura replied, thinking Lance was talking to him. "I don't know how to answer that. . . ."

"How'd you get here?!" Lance continued to ask the pigeons.

"Huh?" Kimura said, still lost. "How did I . . . I'm not telling you anything."

"Stop!" Lance shouted as Lovey and Jeff began to snuggle him. "Get off of me—" Lance kept trying to interrogate Kimura.

"Oh, and you think I won't? TALK!" Lance demanded.

Lance took a step forward for emphasis. However in the process of doing this, he walked right into a glass table. Glass . . . his nemesis.

CRASH!

A lamp from the glass table had toppled over. The lampshade just happened to land perfectly on top of Lance. Not only did the lampshade trap Lance, but it also cast his very bird-y shadow on the wall.

"Hmmm?" Kimura said, confused. He turned,

expecting to find Lance Sterling but instead found a pigeon struggling in a lampshade. Kimura's interest was peaked. He grabbed the frazzled pigeon out of the lampshade.

Kimura poked and prodded Lance. Angry, Lance stabbed Kimura with his sharp beak and Kimura dropped him. But Lance wasn't about to get away so easily. Kimura began to rain down punch after punch. Lance dodged the villain's fists of fury. The flock just sat there and watched.

"All right, Kimura, three ounces of pressure to the vagus nerve. Sleepy night night!" Lance shouted. He karate-chopped Kimura in the neck, using the exact same move that took him out in Japan . . . but this time, nothing happened.

Lance looked pathetically at his wings. "I miss my hands."

With Lance distracted, Kimura swatted him to the floor.

On his back, a defeated Lance sighed. "Lance Sterling is gonna die a pigeon and be buried in a shoebox."

Kimura picked up a stone end table to smash Lance when . . .

ZAP!

Suddenly, Kimura lost all muscle control and flopped to the ground like a pile of human pudding! Lance craned his neck to see Walter in the doorway, multi-pen in hand. The multi-pen had made Kimura all . . . jelly-like.

"Lance, are you okay?" Walter asked, totally freaked out.

Lance was in shock. "Walter?"

Meanwhile, a caravan of Agency SUVs stopped in front of the hotel. Unsurprisingly, Eyes already had the hotel's security feeds on her glasses.

"I hacked the security cams," she reported as she and her team hopped out of the black SUV. "Positive ID on Beckett."

The team was back and ready to take Lance into custody once and for all. They strode into the hotel followed by a backup unit of agents.

"Sterling is here somewhere. I want agents

92

on every exit," she commanded. "And everyone be careful. This is Lance Sterling we're dealing with."

"Tell me where the man with the robotic hand is!" Lanced demanded.

Kimura narrowed his eyes. "Never."

"Boy, I'm about to pigeon wing slap the—" But Lance didn't even finish talking before he slapped Kimura across the face. Jeff, thinking this looked fun, also slapped Kimura. But Kimura just laughed, not all intimidated by these tiny slapping birds.

"Oh, tough guy, okay," Lance said. "Then we do it the hard way. Walter, I need a funnel, jumper cables, and a Nickelback album."

"Nickelback?" Kimura asked, genuinely frightened.

"What? But that would hurt him!" Walter said to Lance.

"That's the whole point!" Lance said.

"I know what to do," Walter replied, making the decision.

Kimura, suddenly nervous, started to plead with Walter. "No, no, no, don't do that."

Walter held up the multi-pen, prepared to use it.

"Oooohoooohooo!" Lance cooed. "That's what I'm talking about, Walter! Go science on this fool!"

"Awww yeah," Walter added, super jazzed. "I'm gonna science all over your face."

Kimura blinked. "Please. Don't."

Walter leaned down close to Kimura and took a deep breath. He pushed one of the pen's tiny buttons, spritzing Kimura in the face.

There was silence, and then Lance spoke. "Did you just give that man a refreshing spritz?"

"It's a truth serum," Walter explained happily. "But, yes, it has a lavender quality to it. Watch." He addressed Kimura directly: "Kimura, what's your biggest secret?"

"I peed in the pool," Kimura sputtered, ashamed.

"That's a lot of honesty," Lance and Walter said in unison.

Lance still thought this was a dumb idea, but he was willing to do anything to find Killian and clear his name. "Who is the guy with the robotic hand?!" Lance asked. "And why is he wearing my face?"

"I . . . I don't know!" Kimura said.

"Then what do you know?" Lance asked.

"Well, I know how to play the flute." Again Kimura was being brutally honest here.

"About the guy with the robotic HAND!" Lance shouted.

"I know he's on his way to Venice right now to steal the agent database," Kimura word-vomited. He sighed. "Ahhh, he's gonna kill me."

"Agent Database?" Walter asked.

"DAH-ta-base," Lance corrected.

"Who says DAH-ta-base?" Kimura said to himself. Apparently Lance did.

Ignoring both of them, Walter pulled up an image of the DAY-ta-base on his watch. "He'll know the identities of everyone at the Agency."

That would not be good. Their covers would be blown, putting every agent in grave danger.

After realizing this, Walter and Lance sat for a moment before they were interrupted by Kimura.

"And once he does, he'll use the Assassin to eliminate all of them."

"Not if I stop him first," Lance said.

"Coo . . . coo, coo."

Lance turned to see Lovey nodding at Kimura's security monitor. Marcy and her crew were charging down the hallway. In another feed showing the lobby, they saw Marcy's agents had the Yakuza already in handcuffs.

"Ugh, she is relentless," Lance said with an exasperated sigh. "Block the door! We need something heavy."

Almost immediately, Lance and Walter's eyes fell on Kimura jiggling on the ground.

Realizing what they were both thinking, Kimura said it loud: "I'm heavy."

Walter and Lance looked at each and nodded. They grabbed Kimura and struggled dragging him toward the door.

"Ooh, cold hands," Kimura said as he

stretched and dragged like a big piece of taffy.

"Are you pulling?!" Lance shouted at Walter.

"Of course I'm pulling!" Walter replied. "Why aren't you pushing? Just put your weight behind it!"

"I am putting my weight! I'm feathers!" Lance said. Kimura's pudding-like body was ominously lurching toward Lance. As if it were able to completely crush him.

CHAPTER
11

JELLY ROLL

O utside the room, Marcy's team was taking their positions around Kimura's hotel room door. But then, they started to hear screaming. Marcy and her team exchanged looks, not sure what to make of it. Shrugging, Eyes used a master hotel key to unlock the door. The agents looked to Marcy. She gave the signal. The door opened a crack, only to instantly slam shut.

"You're out of moves, Sterling," Marcy announced. "You and Beckett are wanted for treason!"

On the other side of the door, Lance was busy extricating himself from under the liquefied Kimura. When he was finally free, he looked out toward the balcony. There sitting on the ledge was the flock! Lovey, Jeff, and the scrawny one with no name.

"We gotta go! Now!" Lance shouted.

"No! Don't leave me like this," Kimura pleaded, watching Lance and Walter run for the balcony.

"Sorry. I'm so sorry," Walter said, looking back at Kimura. At least Kimura wasn't mortally wounded like Lance had planned. He would solidify in a couple of hours.

Lance and Walter ran toward the open balcony door, looking for an escape route. They watched the flock fly from their balcony over to another thirty feet away.

"We gotta get to that balcony," Lance said, immediately understanding what they were trying to tell them. "We're going to have to parkour."

"What??" Walter said.

"Cat pass! Tic Tac! Jelly roll!" Lance said, explaining.

"Desk lamp! Flimflam! Bottlecap! I don't know what any of that means," Walter replied. He could name random things too.

Lance hopped onto Walter's backpack as everyone in the hotel room began to hear beep . . . beep . . . beep . . .

KABOOM!

The door blasted open, and Marcy and her crew toppled to the ground over Kimura. His body jiggled from the impact.

"Ugh!" Marcy exclaimed.

Kimura was, as you would expect, a bit embarrassed. "Hi."

"What the—what happened to you?!" Marcy said, looking at the pile of goo that was Kimura. She began to gag.

"Oh, don't do that," Kimura said. "You're gonna make me . . . HUUUURGGEHH!"

While Kimura and Marcy dry heaved together, Lance and Walter were on the balcony. It was now or never.

"You gotta go!" Lance said to Walter. Marcy and her team still didn't know that Lance was a pigeon. They were going to find Walter here and take him into custody. Walter was a sitting duck here, not Lance.

Walter climbed over the railing, stumbling and sliding along the edge. He cradled pigeon Lance in his arm. Fighting every survival instinct in his body, he curled up on the ledge like a turtle. Not moving.

"Come on, Walter," Lance said. "You can do this. It's a physics problem!"

Suddenly, it dawned on Walter. "It's just basic physics!"

Walter did some quick calculations on his smart watch. It began to project mathematical diagrams of the moves he needed to make in order to get down to the atrium below safely.

"You're right. We can do this!" Walter said, full of confidence.

"Beckett!" Lance and Walter turned to see Marcy charging out onto the balcony.

"We can do this," Walter repeated.

"Beckett, don't you—" Marcy began, reaching forward.

"We're gonna do this!" Walter shouted. "We can do this!!!!"

Marcy barely missed Walter as he leaped off the ledge. He stretched his arm out as far as it could go, reaching for a flagpole. He was going to make it!

But just when it seemed like he was going to grab the flagpole, he fell. Missing it completely.

Lance tumbled after Walter, who was bouncing from balcony to balcony on every floor on the way down.

"Use your gadgets! USE YOUR GADGETS!" Lance yelled.

Good idea! Walter quickly pulled out one of his gadgets and promptly sprayed himself in the face. Nope, that wasn't the right one.

"Ah-ha! Grappling hook!" Walter said, pulling out the right one this time.

The grappling hook sunk into the top of a nearby elevator car, pulling the cable taut.

"Fly! Fly! What am I doing wrong?!" Lance said, flapping his wings but still falling.

Lance landed on Walter's chest and held on for dear life as they swung like Tarzan on a vine.

"AAAAHHHHHHHHH!!!" they cried in unison. The momentum of the grappling hook cable then began to swing them up into the ceiling of the elevator.

SMASH!

Walter and Lance hit the ceiling. Walter fell, crushing Lance under him.

"There he is!" one of Marcy's agents shouted. The elevator rose, dragging Walter and Lance through the crowd of pursuing agents.

"Sorry!!!!!" Walter shouted back as they smashed into the agents. The elevator rose up and up, until Walter and Lance were dangling high above the ground, at the same height as the adjacent elevator's doors. The doors then opened to reveal a large group of agents.

Lance clung to Walter's backpack. He stated the obvious: "Well, that's not good."

"Buenos días . . ." Walter said to the agents sheepishly.

The agents aimed their weapons, ready to take these two jokers down once and for all. But suddenly Walter and Lance's elevator moved again, pulling them up and away!

"Hasta la vista, baby!" Walter called behind him. But just as quickly as the elevator ascended, it descended, dropping Lance and Walter right back to the agents' level.

"Walter, what else you got on that pen?!" Lance demanded.

Walter hit another button on the multi-pen, causing it to become a jet engine, shooting him and Lance off the elevator. Walter and Lance rocketed through the hotel. Unable to hold on to Walter anymore with his tiny bird feet, Lance fell. He landed on a giant pile of towels.

"Oooh, hello, soft landing—" Lance said.

SMACK!

Walter, on the other hand, flew face-first into a statue. His gangly body peeled off and plummeted down toward the hard cement. But the grappling hook was still attached to Lance. As

Walter fell, it caught on the statue, pulling the statue and Lance down after Walter.

"Uh-oh," Lance said. "Walter!"

Thinking fast, Lance dislodged the grappling hook a split second before the statue crashed into the pavement! Lance and Walter continued to fall, tethered together. The tether then hit a palm tree, yanking their free fall to a stop, and released them a few inches off the ground. They landed softly on their feet.

Just when they thought it was all over, agents burst out of the elevators and ran toward Walter and Lance.

"Go! Go! Go!" one shouted.

"There he is," yelled another. "Move!"

"Ugh." Lance groaned. "These guys are the worst."

Walter patted himself down, looking for his multi-pen. He looked up and spotted it on top of a nearby fountain.

"The multi-pen!" Walter said, pointing it out to Lance.

"Yes! Great! Shoot 'em!" Lance responded.

Walter went to grab it when the scrawny bird with no name swooped down out of nowhere and swallowed it whole.

"Well, that is suboptimal," Walter remarked.

"That has a bit of a suck factor to it," Lance added.

As the agents closed in, Walter was ready to defend himself with a pillow he had found.

"Yeah, pillow. Good call," Lance said sarcastically, staring at him.

Then the scrawny bird fluttered down behind them and hiccupped. This actually happened to arm the multi-pen inside his belly!

Walter, recognizing this familiar sound of his pen whirring to life, shouted, "Lance . . . Get down!"

The bird's belly glowed bright pink as Walter and Lance hit the deck. Then a massive stream of rapid-setting foam exploded from his mouth like a fire hose, pinning the agents to the walls.

"Serious string," Walter explained. "Like silly

string, but serious."

Lance surveyed the sticky carnage, impressed. "Oddly effective. C'mon, let's ghost."

Walter and Lance took off, missing Marcy and her team by mere seconds. They charged in only to see their agents covered in goo, hanging off the walls and trees.

"Wow," Ears said. "This is tripped out. This is . . . I don't know what this is."

"This couldn't have been Sterling. No one's even hurt," Marcy said. She knew Lance's style and this . . . wasn't it. She began to look around, trying to piece it all together.

"Might be that kid, Beckett," Ears said.

"That doesn't make sense," Marcy replied. "Beckett is just some nobody in the gadget lab."

"Well, according to his file," Eyes said, pulling up Walter's information on her glasses, "that nobody graduated MIT at fifteen and invented a way to edit human genomes. In middle school."

"Dude is *Jeopardy!* smart," Ear added.

"Well, so are we," Marcy said. She stormed

forward. But she stopped abruptly. "I stepped in it. I stepped in the goo."

Everyone looked down. They were all stuck in the goo.

Ears groaned loudly. "These are my new kicks, man."

COVERT WEAPONS FACILITY, NORTH SEA

Machines were grinding to life in a remote laboratory. An automated assembly line poured molten metal into a large vat as gears turned over and over.

A beyond-stressed weapons lab tech was working on something at his console. Beside him was a giant open window that looked out onto the churning North Sea.

"Oh, I hope this works. I hope this works." He chanted to himself, "Please. Please, please, please."

Suddenly, the evil Killian strolled in, just as the tech finished an adjustment.

"Weapons system online," a computer voice boomed. *"Agent database required for targeting."*

The lab tech gave a giant sigh of relief. He turned to Killian. "It's done!" he said. "The entire facility is running at full capacity." He winced at Killian's lack of enthusiasm, or just lack of reaction for that matter. "Everything is exactly how you wanted it."

Killian walked over and stood silently at the giant window. He looked out on the cold, unforgiving waves crashing against the rock.

"But please . . ." the lab tech continued, "the destruction this is capable of—"

"Since when does your Agency care about the many, many, many lives it destroys?" Killian interrupted. He studied his robot hand, his brow furrowing from a memory he had tried to forget.

Suddenly, a drone yanked the terrified lab tech up into the air and dragged him toward the open window.

"Oh no! Wait! Wait! Wait! No! No! No!

Please! Please, wait!" the lab tech pleaded as he dangled in midair. "You said if I helped you, you'd let me go!"

"Oh yeah, I did. Didn't I?" Killian said.

But he flicked his claw and the drone dropped the lab tech from the overlook. The lab tech's screams fell away with him, to the sea below. Killian strolled away, the drone falling in line behind him.

He gave a wicked grin. "I hear Venice is wonderful this time of year. Think I'll change that."

CHAPTER 12

ANTI-DON'T

Lance's luxury yacht sped across the water. Walter, Lance, and Lovey were on their way to get Killian. On deck, Lance pecked at a GPS screen, showing their course to Venice.

"Aww yeah," Lance said. "Just wait till I get to Venice, I'm gonna tear that fool his own cloaca." He paused for laughter. "Walter."

Walter didn't respond. Lance looked back to see he was working on Lance's antidote from his backpack's mobile lab but also watching his Korean soap opera on his laptop at the same time.

"Walter?!" Lance yelled.

"What?" Walter responded.

"You're still working on that antidote, right?" Lance asked.

"Working on it? In a couple minutes, it's done," Walter said. "But do you know what else is working?"

Lance spoke through his closed beak. "If you say being a pigeon—"

"Being a pigeon!" Walter shouted joyously.

"I'm really gonna throw this boy in the ocean," Lance anger-whispered.

Suddenly, Jeff and the scrawny bird with a multi-pen in its tummy fluttered down from nowhere.

"What? YO! Hey! How did you all get here?" Lance said.

"Jeff and Crazy Eyes aren't going to abandon you," Walter said, finally giving the scrawny bird a name. "They're a part of your flock."

Walter tossed some bread crumbs on the deck, and the birds swooped down eagerly.

"Have some of these," he said. "They're gluten-free."

"You're joking, right? That one ate gum stuck to a tissue," Lance said incredulously.

In between mouthfuls of gluten-free bread, Crazy Eyes hiccupped, arming the pen in his belly. Casually, Walter tapped him on the head, disarming him.

"And a spy pen," Lance added.

"Yeah, we should probably do something about that," Walter said.

Everyone jumped at the sound of Walter's computer alarm. *"Process complete,"* it announced.

"It's ready," Walter said.

"Finally!" Lance shouted, relieved. He watched with anticipation as Walter carefully opened the centrifuge and removed the beaker.

Walter turned around and held his hand out. "May I?"

Lovey cooed sweetly and offered one of her feathers.

"Not this time, Lovey," Walter said. "Thank you."

Walter plucked one from Lance instead.

"OW!" Lance yelped. "Joker . . ."

Walter poured the serum in a beaker and a gurgling black ooze poured out.

"Well, that's not good," Walter said, staring at the black gunk.

Lance was still trying to be optimistic. "'Not good' as in 'it'll taste bad, but still turn me back into a human'?"

"'Not good' as in 'it won't turn you back into a human and if you drink it all your cells will catch on fire,'" Walter explained.

"Come on, man!" Lance said. He was at the end of his rope.

"I'm sorry! I'll figure it out," Walter promised. "Science is all trial and error."

But Lance just looked at his wings, fuming. "This isn't a science lab. If I don't stop this guy, people will die!"

"You don't think I want to stop him too?" Walter shouted back. "Why do you think I'm on this boat? Do you have any idea of how much motion sickness medication I'm on right now? I can hardly feel my legs!" Walter sighed. "But I'm here. Because I believe, together, we can find a good way to stop the bad."

"I know you do, man," Lance said. "But it's a fantasy. When the bad guys hit you, you hit them back, you hit them so hard that they don't get back up. You gotta fight fire with fire."

"When we fight fire with fire, we all get burned. There's no good guys or bad guys, just people," Walter said. Lance winced at his words. Could Walter be right? "And people are worth saving," Walter continued. "Isn't that our job?"

But Lance just looked away, doubling down. "Evil doesn't care that you're nice. I watch good people be taken every day." Lance crossed to the yacht's railing, separating himself from Walter. "But you wouldn't know nothing about that."

Walter's heart broke all over again. His eyes filled with sadness. "You'd be surprised."

He turned and walked back inside to resume working on Lance's antidote.

VENICE, ITALY

From the passenger seat of a little wooden speedboat, Walter stared wide-eyed at the beauty that was Venice.

"First time in Venice?" Lance asked. They hadn't spoken in a while. Walter had been busy working on the antidote, and Lance was focused on formulating his plan to find Killian.

"First time anywhere, really," Walter replied. Lance was starting to realize just how alone Walter was. Lance was actually starting to feel . . . bad for him? He shook his head and saw pigeons flocking in Piazza San Marco from his perch on the yacht.

Walter smiled, pointing toward the famous piazza. "It's always been my dream to come here and feed the pigeons."

"You need help," Lance mocked, this time with a smile. Walter just giggled. As they approached the shore, Lance pointed out a rather unassuming building.

"Time to put your game face on," Lance said. "That's the Agency Data Vault."

But Lance didn't say 'DAY-ta Vault," he said "DAH-ta Vault."

"DAY-ta Vault," Walter corrected.

"If this guy with the robotic hand wants a list of agents, that's where he'll find it," Lance said, ignoring Walter.

While Lance and Walter squabbled about the plan, their speedboat pulled up to the docks. The two turned when they heard a loud click.

"Long way from home, Walter," Marcy said. Marcy, Eyes, and Ears were standing behind them, weapons drawn. "Kimura talked. I know Sterling is here in Venice."

Walter put his hands up. Lance put his wings up.

"Where is he?" Marcy demanded.

"Stay cool," Lance whispered to Walter under his breath.

"I can tell you where he's not," Walter said to

Marcy. "Which is right here."

Lance slowly put his wings down. He took a few steps toward Lovey, Jeff, and Crazy Eyes. He looked like just another pigeon.

"Coo," Lovey said to Lance.

"What? No," Lance replied. "We can't just kill her. That's dark, Lovey."

Marcy looked at Walter, her hard expression softening. "Look, I know you're not a criminal." She lowered her weapon and motioned to her team to do the same. "You're a bright kid. You're inventing things that nobody has ever thought of. I know, because my boot is still stuck in one of them. You're trying to keep the world safe . . . just like your mother did."

Lance's eyes widened. *What's Marcy talking about?* he thought.

"I read your file," Marcy went on, laying the charm on thick. "I know she sacrificed her life to save people." Marcy continued to cajole him. "I can help you, Walter. I can get you your job back. A new lab. All the equipment you need . . ."

Marcy then crouched down to talk to Walter, face-to-face. "Show them what you can do. And no one will ever call you weird again. You just have to give me Sterling."

Lance tensed, honestly unsure of what Walter was going to say. But Walter just looked at Marcy.

"No," Walter said softly. "We should all be working together."

Lance couldn't believe it. Walter was sticking by him. He was actually . . . touched.

But Marcy just shook her head, disappointed. "Bad move, Beckett."

BOOM!

An enormous explosion rocked the entire marina. Everyone turned to see smoke coming from the Agency Data Vault.

"Sterling!" Marcy said, convinced that there could only be one person behind this mayhem. She whipped out a pair of handcuffs and tightened them around Walter's wrists and then to the dock. "Stay here!"

Marcy and her team ran off toward the data vault, positive that they would find their missing double agent. Lance looked around, making sure they were gone, before he hopped over and used his beak to pick the lock on Walter's handcuffs.

"Let's go!" Lance said, locking eyes with Walter. They nodded and took off running toward the DAY-ta vault.

Walter and Lance arrived just in time to see Marcy, her team, and a group of agents surrounding a giant hole in the side of the Agency Data Vault. That explained the explosion. As Marcy and her team stared into the smoking hole, a shape began to emerge. The three of them drew their weapons.

"Freeze!" Marcy shouted. Her eyes widened as the Assassin glided through the haze with the Agency database, an inconspicuous-looking flash drive. The semi-autonomous attack drone had gotten what it was after. It was all over.

"We can't let that thing out of here!" Marcy

shouted. For the first time, there was a faint sound of fear in her voice.

"Open fire!" one of the agents commanded. The agents did as they were told and began to rain down bullets on the Assassin. Lance and Walter ducked behind a column.

"It's already got the database!" Lance said.

"Ohhhh man," Walter said, too scared to care if Lance said "database" right this time. They watched as Marcy and her team tried to contain the Assassin.

"This isn't working!" an agent shouted.

"I'm on it," Ears said. He blasted the Assassin with his sonic weapon. The pulse hit the killer drone, wobbling it slightly. Woo-hoo! But the Assassin recovered and slowly turned its red eye on Marcy and her team. Oh no.

PEW!

The Assassin fired. Marcy and her team dove to safety just in time. But the blast took out the supports of a nearby balcony. It crashed down, trapping Marcy's entire team.

"Let's go!" Lance shouted to Walter. Not stopping to think, Walter grabbed Lance. They ran to the building's stairway, passing Marcy and her team.

"Beckett! Don't you—" Marcy started.

"Don't worry," Walter said. "We'll stop it."

"Beckett!" Marcy shouted back.

"I mean *I'll* stop it because Lance is definitely not here!" Walter said. Phew, that was close. Walter ran up to the roof with Lance in tow. They got to the roof just in time to see the Assassin flying off.

"We can't catch this thing on foot," Walter said.

"Whoa. Hey! Hey! What are you doing?" Lance said as Walter's hands clamped around his pigeon body.

"You're a pigeon, Lance," Walter said, holding Lance up in the air like he was presenting a baby lion on a giant rock. "You're one of the fastest birds in the world."

"No. Put me down, Walter," Lance said, starting to panic.

"You need to fly!" Walter said. "I believe in you!"

"There's another way. Boy, don't you throw me off this roof!" Lance yelled.

Walter threw Lance off the roof, literally pushing the baby bird out of the nest. Lance dropped like a rock.

But Walter was optimistic. "He'll figure it out."

CHAPTER 13

NO MO SOLO

"AHHHHHHHHHH!"

Lance screamed as he tumbled toward the ground.

"Come on! I'm gonna die!" he continued to plummet, just spinning and spiraling, in total panic. Lance saw the ground approaching fast and braced himself.

WHOOSH!

Lance opened his eyes. He wasn't dead. He was . . . flying! His wings were spread out, the wind sailing beneath them. Lance arced directly upward, just before hitting the ground.

"I'm flying . . ." Lance said, stunned. "I'm fly-ing! Ha-ha! I'm flying!"

He looked up in disbelief. But instead of the open sky above him, he saw that he was actually just hanging upside down from Lovey's talons, gliding along.

"Oh," Lance said, a little deflated. "You're flying . . . me." He smiled, looking at Lovey. "Thank you. Good looking out."

She dropped Lance onto a gondola in one of Venice's many water canals. He continued to run, jump, and flap his wings wildly. Still no luck.

Suddenly, Lance's tiny feet were lifted off the gondola. Jeff and Crazy Eyes were holding Lance by the wings and flying along the canal. They were headed toward the Assassin.

"All right, guys! Let's go!" Lance cheered. "We got an Assassin to catch!"

Meanwhile, below, Walter was running through the streets of Venice, darting in and out of crowds.

"Excuse me! Sorry!" Walter shouted. He spotted the flock fly by carrying Lance.

Walter shrugged. "That works too."

Just then, Walter saw a man on a Vespa. That was it!

"This is official business!" he yelled at the confused man. Walter jumped on the Vespa and hit the gas, and the Vespa sped off.

Without him.

Driverless, it smashed right into a wall and exploded.

Walter stared stupidly. Oops. He then spotted another person with a Vespa and ran toward them.

Let's try this again. Walter took the Vespa from the confused driver and shouted (again): "This is official business!"

Up in the air, Lance was riding on Jeff, with Lovey and Crazy Eyes flanking the duo on either side. They were right on the Assassin's tail! The drone was carrying the agent database in his claws.

"We need to get that database," Lance said to his flock. "Any ideas?"

ON A MISSION

Lance Sterling is on a mission to retrieve a stolen weapon from a famous dark web broker named Katsu Kimura. When Joyless demands that he wait for a backup team, Lance scoffs.

"TEAM? I FLY SOLO."

"UH-OH. TIME TO INTRODUCE MYSELF."

Lance is inside a giant fish tank when he spots Kimura handing stolen tech over to his buyer.

The glass shatters, and he surfs over on a massive wave!

"HEY, HEY, DON'T TAKE THE LOSS SO HARD. I MEAN, YOU DID GREAT. AND YOU GOT TO MEET **LANCE STERLING."**

In one totally epic move, Lance launches himself into the sky to retrieve the stolen tech. Using his wing suit, this superspy is able to soar all the way back to headquarters— in style!

BACK AT THE AGENCY . . .

Lance decides to visit the lab tech guys. The latest spy tech he's gotten from these guys has been a bit . . . weird. Like a kitty glitter bomb! He meets Walter Beckett, a smart kid with a knack for inventing unique spy tech.

"UHH. HI. WOW. UHH, I'M WALTER BECKETT. PLEASURE TO MEET YOU!"

Lance doesn't need help from anyone—that is, until he is forced to go on the run from Internal Affairs agent Marcy and her team, who think he is working for the bad guys. He jumps in his spy car and races over to the one person who can help him.

"I NEED TO DISAPPEAR."

When Lance arrives at Walter's house, he demands that Walter help him disappear. Walter is surprised to see the world's greatest spy in his grandma's house.

"AHHHHH! WHOAH! WHA—HOW DID YOU? WHAT ARE YOU DOING IN MY . . . WHAT'S UP?"

Lance accidentally drinks the formula Walter has been developing. Walter is horrified.

Before Lance knows what hit him, he is transformed into a pigeon! He is not happy, to say the least. He is even more unhappy when Walter's pet pigeon, Lovey, tries to nuzzle him.

"STOP, GIRL! COME ON!"

With a new flock, Lance must face his enemies head on. Lance learns to work as part of a team, and ultimately, he proves his innocence. Lance discovers that friendship is the most powerful spy tech of all . . .

AND THAT IS COO!

Crazy Eyes gave a loud belch. The multi-pen in his tummy began to glow.

"Ooh, I like how you think," Lance said, smiling. He hit Crazy Eyes on the head, causing him to zap the Assassin with a bolt of electricity! Wobbling from impact, the Assassin dropped the flash drive.

"Bull's-eye!" Lance cheered. Lovey and Jeff swooped down, placing Lance right in the falling flash drive's path.

"Got it!" Lance said, the flash drive dropping perfectly in his wings.

The flock veered away. But the Assassin wasn't going to let them go that easily. The drone circled back, firing down at the pigeons.

"Yeah, I didn't think he'd like that," Lance said.

The Assassin fired again, zapping Lance's tiny foot. He dropped, letting go of the flash drive. It began to tumble down, down, down . . . until Crazy Eyes nabbed it! He tossed the flash drive to Lovey, who caught it with her feet. The pigeons were having fun.

"Oh, that's right, y'all like games," Lance said, picking up on this. "Let's play some keep-away. Go long!"

Lovey tossed the flash drive back to Crazy Eyes. Lance cheered them on from Jeff's back as the fluffy bird flew the two of them through a series of clotheslines. But Lance came too close to a line and was tangled up in hanging laundry! Jeff continued to fly as Lance hung, stuck on the line.

Lance managed to free himself from the clothes and began to fall, only to land right on top of the Assassin! Knowing that he could swerve the drone side to side while on its back, Lance held on to the Assassin as it screamed through the sky.

The pigeons continued to toss the flash drive back and forth to each other, avoiding shots from the Assassin. This wasn't hard to do, as the drone was having trouble aiming with Lance riding on its back.

"Ha-ha!" Lance jeered at the Assassin. "Not

so easy, is it, Roomba?!"

Lance saw his chance to get out of there and dove off the Assassin and back onto Jeff. Jeff threw the flash drive to Lovey.

"Lovey! All you, girl!" Lance shouted, Jeff flying the both of them ahead. "Hit me! I'm open!" Lovey tossed the flash drive to Lance.

"I got it! I got it!" Lance cheered, and then . . . "Oh no!"

Lance found himself flying through an old lady's apartment—destroying the kitchen table. Blissfully unaware, the old lady barely blinked and calmly stirred her tea as Jeff and Lance turned down her hallway. Lance couldn't hold on any longer and let go, hitting the floor of the hallway hard. Just then, the drone smashed into the hallway wall and spotted Lance. With the drone hot on his tail, Lance ran down the hall. Glancing up at a window, he saw the flock outside. Right where he needed them!

Lance jumped out the window, the momentum carrying him across an alley to another building. But the Assassin continued to chase him, gaining on him. Inside the building, the game of keep-away continued as Lance dodged and weaved. He was in full spy mode, narrowly escaping the Assassin at every turn.

"Oh, no, no, no, no," Lance said, the Assassin dangerously close. "This is about to suck!"

It was over. The Assassin had closed in on him. It fired, blowing Lance out through a skylight and onto the roof. The impact caused Lance to slip. He dropped the flash drive. It disappeared off the ledge of the roof.

"No!" Lance cried.

Without a second thought, Lance jumped off the ledge, tucked his wings back, and dove like a skydiver.

The flash drive plummeted toward the canal below. The Assassin rocketed after it as well . . . closing in faster than Lance.

"C'mon, c'mon, c'mon, c'mon!" Lance said, trying to make himself go faster.

The Assassin was about to grab it until . . . a

Vespa-driving Walter sped into view on the foot-bridge. Walter stretched his arm out over the canal and caught the flash drive!

Going way too fast, the Assassin couldn't slow itself down and smashed through a gondola and then into the water below. Lance landed on Walter's Vespa. He looked up at Walter, amazed.

"Catch of the century!" Lance shouted, still in disbelief.

"I've never caught anything in my whole life!" Walter said, also amazed.

Walter and Lance started up the Vespa again, which clattered down a set of stairs. Walter, still having some trouble controlling it, readjusted his grip and began to speed off toward the piazza.

"Wooo-hooo!" Lance cheered, giving Walter a big wing five.

"That was amazing! We did it!" Walter said.

"We're going to talk about you throwing me off that roof, though!" Lance said.

"Yeah, I really thought that would work out better!" Walter replied honestly.

Lance brushed it off. "Nah, it's cool. It's cool. We're gonna holler about it in a minute. I'm gonna let you have this moment."

"Whoo!" Walter said, still on a high. "We're unstoppable!"

But then, a robotic hand appeared out of nowhere, punching Walter and sending Lance and the Vespa flying into the middle of the square.

Walter's ears rang, his vision blurred from the massive punch. When his vision began to clear, he saw a shadowy figure walking up behind him. Thinking quickly, Walter reached for the flash drive, but the figure's robot hand grabbed it first.

"Ah, ah, ah—that belongs to me," Killian said.

"Technically, it belongs to the United States government," Walter spat back. He tried to stand, but Killian's foot stomped down on his chest, pinning him to the ground. Killian just smiled darkly.

"Lance! LANCE!" Walter called.

"Sterling?" Killian asked. He smirked and

called out to the missing superspy. "What do you say, Lance? Come out and we'll have some good fun. You're the hero, right? The spy who saves the day. Destroying anybody that stands in your way . . . Oh, I'd love to have some fun."

Walter struggled to get away, hoping he could slip away and find Lance. But Killian stomped him to the ground again.

"Guess he's not coming," Killian said.

Lance was only slowly coming to. When he realized what was happening, he pulled his way out from under the wrecked Vespa.

"No," Lance said, woozy.

"Ah, life is full of disappointment," Killian said to Walter. With that, the villain aimed his robo-hand at Walter. It was all about to be over.

"You don't have to do it this way," Walter said weakly. "It won't make anything better."

Watching this, Lance tried to wrestle himself free, but his foot was stuck beneath the Vespa.

"No. No!" Lance said, straining to free himself. "WALTER!"

Killian turned sharply at the sound of Lance Sterling's voice. This distraction gave Walter an opportunity to reach into his pocket. He threw something that looked like crumbs all over Killian.

"Bread crumbs??" Killian asked, looking down at himself. Almost instantaneously, pigeons from all over the piazza snapped to attention.

Walter smiled, knowing they had won. He turned on his cool-guy voice. "They're gluten-free."

Killian's eyes went wide as he turned to see EVERY pigeon in the piazza descend on him! Lance and Walter watched as the birds enveloped Killian in a writhing, feathery bird-nado.

"Lance! Let's go!" Walter called out. They took off running, and when the cloud of pigeons scattered, Lance and Walter were gone.

"Hold it right there!" Marcy shouted. Wait, Marcy?!

Marcy, Eyes, and Ears were standing right behind Killian.

"Turn around. Nice and slow," Marcy commanded Killian.

Ominously, Killian smiled, doing as he was told. But it wasn't Killian who turned around, it was . . . Lance?! Killian had some sort of advanced-tech mask he was using. It was making everyone think Lance was behind all this! Marcy didn't see that it was a mask. All she saw was Lance's face.

"Hands where I can see them," Marcy said.

But fake Lance only raised one of his arms.

"Both hands," Marcy said through gritted teeth.

Fake Lance suddenly swiveled his robotic hand.

Before everyone could react, Ears began to hear something on his headphones.

"Watch out!" he shouted, pushing Marcy and Eyes out of the way as the Assassin rocketed past them. Casually, fake Lance latched onto the Assassin. It flew off with him . . . and the agent database.

"Did anybody else see that Agent Sterling had . . . ?" Eyes said, trailing off.

"A robot hand," Ears finished.

Marcy's face fell, filling with confusion. "Yeah."

Lance and Walter had been running for a while. They finally reached the dock and boarded Lance's yacht. It turned out that the yacht was not only a luxurious boat, but it also had a secret submarine for emergencies. And this was an emergency.

Lance and Walter sat in the cockpit of the yacht's mini-sub, processing what had just happened.

Walter began to pace around on an adrenaline high. "That was totally crazy. When he had his foot on my head, I was like, 'Aaah!' And you were like, 'NOOOO!' And then I was like, 'Bread crumbs!'"

"He still got away with the database," Lance reminded Walter.

"Oh, did he?" Walter pressed. "Or DID he? *Orrr did he*?"

Lance stared at Walter, deadpan. "I feel

like you want me to say 'What are you talking about?'"

"Oh, I'll tell you what I'm talking about. During the whole bird-nado thing . . . I put a tracker on him!" Walter announced. He activated a screen on the sub console. Lance saw a tiny blip pinging.

"Wait. That's him? That's Robo-hand?" Lance asked.

"Yup," Walter said.

"Yes! YES! My man! Oh, there is no way I could've done this without you, Walter!" Lance shouted.

Walter was dumbfounded. "What? What?"

"What?" Lance asked.

"What did you say?" Walter asked again.

"I think I said . . ." Lance began.

"You said you couldn't have done it without me," Walter said.

Walter grabbed Lance and hugged him tight. Lance tensed at first but then relaxed, letting himself be hugged for a second. It had been a long day. But, wait, did Walter think they were a

137

team? But . . . Lance Sterling flew solo! Lance tried to pull away.

"All right. Okay. We reached the time limit on this, Walter," Lance said, resisting the hug. "All right. Hey, will you stop? You're squeezing too—OOOHHHH! Whoa."

PLOP!

Something had just come out of Lance. Lance and Walter looked down, staring at an . . . egg? Lance had just laid an egg.

Lance broke the stunned silence. "Walter, what happens in the submarine stays in the submarine."

"You just laid an egg," Walter said, processing. He gasped. "YOU LAID AN EGG!"

"It just kinda slipped out, man," Lance said, trying to explain.

But Walter wasn't judging. He had just realized something very important. This was a game changer. "You just laid an egg, Lance! This is amazing! Do you not realize what this means? YOU'RE A GIRL!"

"Oh! Excuse me?!" Lance said.

Walter slapped his forehead. "Of course! Of course! That's why I couldn't figure this out! I used Lovey's DNA in the serum!"

Walter cracked open his mobile science lab.

"And that helps us how?" Lance asked, trying to piece it together.

"Because," Walter said, "now all I need to do is change one variable in the antidote . . ."

Walter fiddled with his equipment. He made one last adjustment and hit a timer.

". . . and you'll be human again," Walter announced.

Lance nearly doubled over with relief. "I'm gonna be me!"

But these words from Lance triggered something in Walter, curbing his excitement. Walter realized what this could potentially mean. It meant that his new friend was going to be Lance Sterling again.

"Unless, you know . . . maybe you want to stay a pigeon a little longer," Walter said.

Lance gave Walter a look that said, *Seriously*?

"Right! Of course," Walter said, understanding. "One antidote coming right up."

"Director Jenkins, we lost the database," Marcy said to Joyless. Eyes and Ears were behind her, searching the abandoned yacht. "Every Agency employee is compromised. You need to pull everyone in for their own safety."

"And you're sure it was Lance?" Joyless said, feeling the weight of this news.

"Yes," Marcy said. But then rethought it. "Maybe?" She sighed. "Okay, I don't know what I saw. But I still know for a fact that Sterling came here on this boat."

"Sterling wasn't on this boat," Eyes announced behind Marcy.

"Come on!" Marcy said to her team. "There's got to be something! A footprint? A candy wrapper? Some overpriced face lotion because there is no way that his skin looks that good without help?!"

"Look, everything is comin' up blank," Ears said.

"If Sterling was on this boat, he didn't leave a fingerprint, his lips never touched a glass, and somehow he didn't have feet," Eyes said.

Marcy was stunned.

"I think it's safe to say your investigation isn't getting anywhere," Joyless said.

Just then, something caught Marcy's eye. She picked up a blue bird feather, twirling it in her fingers.

BOOM!

A flash of a chemical reaction shone from Walter's mobile lab. Walter leaned back and stared at the beaker of serum he just concocted. He placed it in front of Lance, nodding.

Lance looked at the beaker, then at the world around him. Walter, the other pigeons . . . it would never look like this again. He then took a steadying breath and downed the serum.

Lance experienced the transformation

through his pigeon vision. In 360, he could see Lovey, Jeff, Crazy Eyes, and Walter. They were all watching him. Finally, Lance's vision began to narrow like curtains closing on a stage. His vision was reduced to human vision . . . then his eyes closed completely. In Lance's bloodstream, one by one, the blue blood cells became red as the switches in his body's DNA flipped back to human.

"Lance . . ." It was Walter. He was staring at Lance.

Lance was on his hands and knees, breathing hard. He was human again!

"Lance?" Walter called out again. Lance looked up at Walter.

"Did it work?" Lance asked. He started to get up and promptly bumped his head on the ridiculously low ceiling of the submarine.

"Whoa. Okay, take it easy," Walter said, rushing to his side.

Lance rubbed his head and saw his hands. Human hands.

"I got my hands back," Lance said in disbelief. "Yes. YES! My pecs! My pectoral muscles. My abdominalia. Oh, Walter! You. Are. A . . ." Lance grabbed Walter and kissed him. "I could do that cuz I got lips now."

Lance laughed. Then realized something. "I'm naked. Little bit awkward."

"Lucky for you, and for me, I planned ahead," Walter said, handing him a tux.

Lance put his tux on, like he had done for years, but this time it was different. This time, he appreciated every shoe, belt, and cuff link. Finally, Lance straightened his bow tie. He was in full uniform. He was Lance Sterling again.

"There he is!" Walter cheered. "Lance Sterling back in action!"

But the flock looked sad as Lance tugged his jacket straight. Their new bird friend was gone.

The GPS's voice cut through the silence. *"You have arrived at your destination."*

Walter and Lance both turned and looked out the submerged window. Walter's eyes widened as the sub rose to the surface.

"All right, bad guy," human Lance said, smiling. "I'm coming for you."

CHAPTER
14

BOOM

UNCHARTED ISLAND, NORTH SEA

Lance stepped onto shore. Finally human again, he was ready to take down this bad guy and clear his name.

"Okay, the evil dude is a mile due west," Walter said, following Lance and looking at the tracker on his watch. "So what's the plan, partner? I've got plenty of glitter, yay-palm . . . A splat-a-pult."

Lance didn't even look up when he spoke. "No."

"No what?" Walter asked.

"I'm taking it from here, Walter," Lance said.

Walter looked back at him, stunned.

"Look, lives are on the line," Lance said. "I've got this now."

"You've got this?" Walter repeated. "But . . . we're a team. You said so yourself—"

"And you did your job. You un-birded me. Now it's time to do things my way." Lance powered up the weapons in his tux.

"That's wrong. You're so wrong," Walter said. He held up his backpack. "Look, I've got everything that we—"

"This is not the place for your weird gadgets," Lance said.

"Weird?" Walter's heart sank.

"Go home," Lance said.

Walter was hurt but defiant.

"No," Walter said. "I'm not giving up."

PHOOM!

Lance shot Walter in the neck with a tranq dart.

A look of shock and confusion passed over Walter's face. "Lance?" He held his neck, looking back at Lance. Walter dropped into the submarine chair, woozy. "Why?"

"I can't lose any more good people," Lance replied.

145

But Lance had nothing left to say. He shut the submarine's canopy and shoved the sub away from shore. Lance watched the sub submerge, mourning the loss of his one and only friendship. But he did what he had to do. He closed his eyes in resolve.

"I fly solo."

Lance Sterling was back in action. He climbed up over a rocky outcropping to get the lay of the land. He saw an entrance to a fortified complex. Killian's lair. He took one last look behind him. No sign of Walter. Lance felt a pang of regret. But pushing those feelings down, he headed toward the ruined manor house.

The Assassin floated up from a giant open crater in the middle of the ruins. Lance took cover as it scanned for intruders. As the Assassin flew off, Lance emerged from his hiding spot and dropped down into the crater it came out of.

Lance slinked through the cold industrial hallways of the secret military complex beneath the manor house. When . . .

BOOF!

Lance walked right into a glass door. It must have been some latent avian behavior. He shook it off and kept going. Eventually, the corridor opened up into a vast industrial area. The factory. Lance was headed for the factory, when suddenly the Assassin appeared again out of nowhere!

It had found him.

Killian was relaxing in his office, when . . .

THUNK!

The broken remains of the Assassin landed at his feet.

"I think that's yours. But that *face* you've been using is mine," Lance said, stepping out of the shadows. "Database isn't gonna do you any good with your fancy toy messed up like that."

"You really thought I was going to use one drone to take out every name on this list?" Killian said, holding up the database flash drive.

"I mean, I did. Until you asked that question

that way. Casts a little doubt," Lance said.

"Tell me, Agent Sterling . . ." Killian said. "You managed to stop one drone. How do you plan on stopping one thousand?"

Killian slammed the flash drive into his console. Energy coursed through a series of high-tech connectors. Lance's eyes watched the wave of electricity flow through to the factory floor below, where hundreds of drones began to hum to life. One by one their red eyes lit up.

As the drones processed data from the flash drive, the faces of agents popped up on their LED screens.

Lance's eyes went wide in horror. He turned to Killian, only to feel a sharp pain in his neck. It was a dart. Lance lunged at Killian, but a powerful electric shock surged from the dart, knocking him to the ground.

Killian smiled. "Sleepy night night."

When Lance came to, he discovered he was in some kind of control room. Video feeds of various locations played on multiple screens.

Killian's voice slithered from the shadows. "It won't be long now. Do you feel that dread? Ooh, can you feel it? Rolling around you like a fog."

"I told you. I don't even know you, man," Lance said.

"But I know you. Think about it," Killian said. "No? I'll give you a little bit of help. *Kyrgyzstan.*"

Lance's eyes widened, remembering.

"Awww, he remembers! I mean, I certainly never forgot that day. You were magnificent. You were a one-man army. Lot of witty catch-phrases, and you had all these fancy toys that just went BOOM!" Killian said. He showed Lance his scarred face.

"You were a bunch of bad dudes about to hurt a lot of innocent people. And it's my job to keep everyone safe," Lance replied.

Killian was enraged. "Everyone? I watched EVERY SINGLE ONE of my people die as your Agency's weapons rained down on us. You took everything from me!"

He quickly collected himself, then smiled. "And you know the rules. You hit me hard, Sterling. I hit back harder."

Killian turned to Lance and raised his robot arm. Behind him, on the factory floor, hundreds of Assassins rose in response. The glass window opened, and with a flick of his wrist, he launched the drones. The Assassins flew off like a plague of locusts. On one of the screens, a flashing dot representing the Assassins inched closer to a target—Agency headquarters.

Killian pressed his neck, activating the holographic Lance mask.

"All of this . . ." Killian said disguised as Lance, ". . . because of you."

Suddenly, there was a beeping on the screen and flashing letters: "INBOUND VEHICLE."

Killian clicked off the Lance mask and crossed to the screen. It was Walter's submarine.

"He's coming back for me," Lance said to himself, horrified.

"Aww, one of your little mates coming to the

rescue," Killian taunted.

"Walter, no," Lance whispered, his face filling with dread.

Killian flashed a sinister grin. "Why didn't you tell me you invited your friend?"

"No, no, no. No. Okay . . ." Lance sputtered.

"I would have set out another chair," Killian said, dragging Lance's chair over to the window.

"Hey. This kid is harmless," Lance said. "He doesn't have anything to do with this, okay."

Killian didn't say another word.

"We can figure this out," Lance said desperately. "Look at me. Look at me. I'm sorry, all right?"

Killian flicked his hand, and an Assassin zoomed out over the ocean.

"There's another way," Lance said.

Killian gestured with a claw, and the Assassin dove into the water.

"Do you hear me?!" Lance screamed. "DO NOT hurt this kid! Don't—don't do this! Please!"

The Assassins fired at the submarine. An

explosion blasted out of the water. The submarine and everything inside of it was destroyed.

Lance could only look on . . . horrified.

"I'm taking everything from you," Killian said.

Killian walked out of the office, leaving Lance alone.

Completely alone.

Lance was slumped over in the chair, broken. He was racked with grief and guilt over Walter.

But suddenly he heard a faint flapping noise. Lance looked up, thinking he was just imagining things. Jeff, Crazy Eyes, and Lovey gently fluttered down on either side of him. He was floored. Then Lance—sensing a presence—slowly turned his head to see Walter standing in the doorway.

"Walter! But I saw . . . How did you . . . ?" Lance sputtered.

Walter tossed Lance a pre-deployed inflatable hug.

"Oh, you know, one of my weird gadgets," Walter said.

The inflatable hug popped open in Lance's lap.

"The inflatable hug," Lance said, smiling. "I thought I lost you, man."

"I'll always have your back, Lance," Walter said. "That's what it means to be a team. It's something I learned a long time ago."

"From your mom?" Lance asked.

Walter smiled.

"You're a good friend, Walter," Lance said.

Walter wrapped Lance in a giant hug.

"Hey. I'm sorry for shooting you in your neck," Lance said.

"I'm sorry for the cloaca," Walter replied. Then he got back to the mission at hand. "So what's your plan to stop this guy?"

"Nope. Not my plan," Lance said. "Time to do it your way."

"My way . . ." Walter said.

"Oh yeah. We're about to Walter-ize this thing," Lance said.

Walter beamed proudly. "Well, in that case, we're going to need a bigger flock." He tapped a

153

message on his watch.

"You're calling Marcy, aren't you?" Lance said.

"Yup," Walter replied.

Lance smiled awkwardly. "Tell her I said hey."

Walter sent off the message. Then he held up Crazy Eyes like a gun and bonked him on the head. A seltzer-like stream shot out of his mouth, freezing Lance's manacles. Lance pulled up, shattering them.

Just then, the monitor beeped loudly, showing the swarm of Assassins fast approaching Agency headquarters.

Lance turned to Walter. "Let's get weird."

Walter dropped an invisible mic.

"Boom."

CHAPTER
15

COME ON, BIRDS!

Lance burst through a door and ran down the hall trying to find his way out. As he made his way outside, he was suddenly cut off by an Assassin. Another Assassin zipped in behind him.

"No where to run from this, Lance," Killian's voice echoed from nowhere.

"Listen, I'm sorry about what happened in Kyrgyzstan," Lance said. He turned to see Killian emerging from the shadows. "But we are stuck in the good guy/bad guy vortex. We do not have to do it like this."

"Yeah, bit late for that," Killian replied.

"It's not. We're both just people who've made

mistakes. We can work this out," Lance said. He looked out of his peripheral and saw Walter, scooting behind a crumbling wall, tapping at his watch, trying to hack into Killian's robotic hand that controlled the drones. But it wasn't connecting. Walter spoke into a headset: "Got it! I'm connected!"

"Nobody else has to get hurt," Lance said, trying to keep Killian talking. If Killian was distracted, Lance could move him closer to Walter to get his robotic hand in range of the watch.

Killian was fuming; he knew this was some kind of trick. "You should know better than anyone. Someone always gets hurt."

"Not today," Lance said. He tossed a sticky audio blaster, like he used in Japan, against the wall and hit Play on his new "GET WEIRD" playlist. A song blared.

"You brought your own soundtrack," Killian remarked.

"We like to make an entrance." Lance smirked. Behind him, POOF! Kitty glitter exploded!

"Huh," Killian said, distracted by the kitty glitter. "Awww . . ."

Suddenly, the pigeons broke through the cloud of glitter, and they were ready for battle. Jeff and Lovey had some of Walter's gadgets clipped on their wings. Crazy Eyes cocked himself like a shotgun, and the multi-pen inside him started glowing. They unleashed an attack on the Assassins! Jeff and Lovey cruised over like bombers. Crazy Eyes blasted some others with an electric charge.

Then a powerful sonic blast knocked some of the Assassins off course. Killian turned to see Marcy jumping off the top of the ruined manor and riding an Assassin to the ground. Her crew was behind her, taking on the Assassins. One of the Assassins ricocheted off the wall, knocking Killian to the ground. His face glitched, flickering the Lance mask on and off.

"Would you look at that," she said. "There's a man with a robot hand wearing your face who took the M-9 Assassin." Marcy landed next to

Lance. "I guess I owe you an apology."

"Okay. Go ahead," Lance said.

"No. That was it. That was the apology," Marcy replied.

"Oh! I accept." Lance smiled.

Unfazed, Killian raised his arm to call forward a swarm of Assassins. "I'm gonna make this hurt!"

He waved his claw, and the Assassins closed in on the heroes.

"Look out!" Eyes shouted.

The Assassins dove, the pigeons took to the air, and Marcy and Lance rolled to cover. Walter hunkered down behind the ruins and tapped furiously at his watch.

"Walter hacked his hand," Lance explained to Marcy. "We've got to buy him some time to shut down the drones!"

"Got it! What kind of firepower we talkin'?" Marcy said.

Lance tossed a bag of strange-looking weaponry to Marcy. "Just go along with it."

Then he grabbed the binder bubbles weapon and charged out at Killian.

"Take your best shot," Killian said. Lance struck him with it, but Killian sent him flying to the dirt.

"This one sucks," Lance said.

Walter was still uploading the hack on his watch, and he saw Lance hit the wall. "No, no, no," Walter said in his earpiece to Lance. "That's binder bubbles! Push the button on the back!"

Lance hit the button and the weapon bloomed open and launched a flurry of bubbles as Killian's drones unloaded missiles. The bubbles floated up and captured them. The missiles exploded in the bubbles that contained them—just wiggling from the mini-blast inside.

Killian's eyes went wide, as did Marcy's.

"BUBBLES?!" Killian shouted.

Marcy turned to Lance. "Oh, you gotta let me try that." She began to run, holding a glowing orb.

"That's a collide-a-scope," Walter said in

Marcy's earpiece. "Throw it!"

She hurled the orb at Killian, who caught it.

The orb opened and a little "Smile" bulb rose and FLASH! Killian was blinded. Then the world became a kaleidoscope of color and refracted images. Marcy seemed to be coming at him from every angle.

"This stuff is amazing!" Marcy shouted. WHAM! She leveled Killian with a kick.

Then Crazy Eyes and Jeff landed on Killian. Crazy Eyes spit up a Band-Aid onto his face, while Jeff pigeon-slapped him.

Walter's hands popped up from his hiding hole and released a squadron of pigeons armed with gadgets. "Splat-a-pult! Prism spray! Hypno-stars! Snorepedo! Scream team!" Walter shouted.

One of the pigeons dropped a flash drive labeled "FAVORITE SCREAMS" into Ears's hands.

"Well, what've we got to lose?!" Eyes said to Ears.

Ears shrugged and loaded it into his weapon.

He fired and Walter's "EEEEOOWWWW EEEOOOOWWW" blasted.

"Six o'clock!" Eyes shouted. "Ears blasts a drone!"

"Half past two!" Eyes commanded again. Ears blasted another. Eyes noticed drones coming from every direction and winced. "Four thirty! Quarter past five!" The drones went haywire, crashing into each other and exploding into walls.

Marcy continued to use Walter's gadgets to take down incoming drones when a laser shot, courtesy of Lovey, zipped right past Marcy's head, hitting a drone behind her.

Marcy gave her a thankful nod. "Nice shot!" she said.

Lovey rolled her eyes. "Coo."

"Thank you?" Marcy replied.

Meanwhile, Lance was running out of gadgets to use. "Walter, gonna need a reload, buddy."

"Ask and you shall receive." Walter said over the earpiece.

"Are those pigeons wearing tiny backpacks?"

Killian asked, confused.

More pigeons flew in, dropping small colored squares on the ground. On impact they turned into a massive geyser of color, shooting into the sky and taking out drones.

Lance smiled and nodded. "That's hot! We need more of those!"

"I call it Fifty Shades of Yay!" Walter said excitedly.

Killian was surrounded in a rainbow cloud. "ARGHHH! Come on, now!"

With one final burst of energy, Killian lunged at Lance. Lance struggled with Killian, who punched him twice and then threw him to the dirt, next to the wall that Walter was crouching behind. Walter watched the progress bar on his watch climb to 60 percent.

"Walter! My face can't take much more of this," Lance shouted.

"You keep doing your thing and I'll do mine!" Walter assured him.

"Yeah, well, your thing seems to be a lot

easier than my thing!" Lance said.

"We have different skill sets! That's what makes us such a great team!" Walter replied.

Lance ran back into battle while Crazy Eyes fired serious string at Killian, sticking his robo-hand to the wall. Killian groaned in frustration and managed to direct a drone to blast him free. Rubble from the wall hit Crazy Eyes, sending him flying—the multi-pen coming free and blasting a green cloud, which floated down over the battle-field.

Marcy had Killian in headlock, when she sneezed right in his face.

"Excuse me. Phew," she said. "Why do I smell lavender?"

"Uh-oh." Walter said. "Truth serum."

Marcy, Lance, and Killian were all under the influence of the truth serum.

"I have five cats each named after a member of the New Kids on the Block," Marcy blurted out.

"Oh, I love New Kids," Lance said.

"Jon, Joey, Jordan, Donnie, and Danny," Marcy replied.

"I really want to hurt you right now," Killian said unsurprisingly. He grabbed a detached drone weapon and fired at them. He missed, but the blast disintegrated the wall Walter was hiding behind.

Killian glared at Walter, realizing. "You! What . . . what are you doing?!"

"I'm not telling you anything!" Walter shouted.

"I'll tell you what he's doing," Lance said, still under the truth serum. "He's gonna hack into your claw and shut down your drones!"

Uh-oh.

Deciding it was better to live to fight another day, Killian threw his robotic hand up, and an Assassin zoomed in, flying him up and away.

Walter looked down at his watch, now at 90 percent. He was losing the signal as Killian got farther away and out of range. He grabbed the multi-pen and shot a stream of serious string at Killian. The string stuck to Killian's foot. Walter tried to tether Killian to the ground so he could finish hacking the Assassins, but the Assassin carrying Killian yanked Walter into the air instead.

Lance saw Walter get pulled up into the air. "No. No!"

"I'm coming, Walter!" Lance shouted, dodging the assassins. Lance grabbed Walter's backpack just in time. He held on to the banister. Walter checked the progress bar on his watch. It was close. They needed to shut down the drones fast or the entire Agency would be done for.

"Almost there!" Walter shouted to Lance. "Don't let go! Please don't let go!"

"I got you!" Lance said, fighting to hold on, but the backpack straps broke and Walter was pulled away. Lance watched in horror as Killian rocketed straight up into the air with his one true friend. "WALTER!!!!"

Lovey landed on Walter's broken-up backpack. Lance spotted the vial of serum sticking out. He knew what he had to do.

Meanwhile, in the air, Killian looked down to see Walter dangling below him. He sliced into the serious string, but it was just a sticky mess. Walter's feet dangled in the air as the island got smaller and smaller beneath them. Killian began to reel Walter in.

"Come on, come on, come on, come on . . ." Walter said as the progress bar on his watch climbed to 96 percent . . . 97 percent . . . 99 percent . . . . Walter spun around and was now face-to-face with Killian.

100 percent and BEEP! The watch blinked the question: "DEACTIVATE DRONE? Y/N."

"If you shut them down now, you'll kill us both!" Killian said to Walter.

Walter looked at the drop below him and went white.

"And you're not a killer," Killian reminded him.

Walter steeled himself. "No. I'm a hugger." Walter stuck a button-sized device onto Killian.

PHWOOM!!

The inflatable hug inflated around Killian, splitting him and Walter apart.

As Walter toppled through the air, he

remembered his mother's words of encourage-
ment from his childhood: *"One day, your gadgets
are going to keep the world safe."*

He hit the button on his watch—BEEP!—he
deactivated the Assassins. The Assassin carrying Killian shut down and began to fall. Killian, in
the inflatable hug, fell too.

Assassins dropped like flies around the
island. Marcy looked up. But it wasn't over.

A thousand feet aboveground, Walter flipped
and flopped through the air, eyes filled with ter-
ror. Then, backlit by the sun, descending like
some mythical creature out of the heavens . . .
was LANCE THE PIGEON.

And pigeon Lance was flying! Gliding and
flapping through the clouds he swooped in and
managed to grab Walter's shirt.

"I've got you, Walter!" Lance said. But Lance
struggled to maintain control, then straightened
out, tucked his wings, and dove toward Walter.

"Lance, it's okay! It's okay. You can't do this
alone," Walter shouted.

He flapped furiously but couldn't slow Walter down.

"I'm not alone," Lance said, straining. Suddenly, Lovey, Crazy Eyes, and Jeff flew and latched onto Walter too.

"Come on, birds!" Lance commanded as the other pigeons swooped in to help. "Fly!!"

The combined bird-power didn't stop Walter's fall, but it slowed it. Walter and the birds smashed through a broken wall of the ruined manor and bounced to the ground, dust and feathers everywhere.

Lance was battered and hurt but pulled himself up to Walter. Walter was unconscious.

"Walter? Walter?!!" Lance said.

Walter finally opened his eyes and groaned. He was alive.

"What does internal bleeding feel like?" Walter asked weakly.

"This," Lance said. "It feels like this."

"Come here," Walter said, both friends reaching for a hug. They stopped—too many broken bones.

"No, no. No hugs!" Lance said. "You'll make me lay an egg or something in front of Marcy." Lance raised a bent wing. "I think I need a vet."

"Once I can move again, I'll turn you back into a man," Walter promised.

Marcy rushed up to them. "Sterling. You're a bird?!"

"Hey, Marcy," Lance said, trying to sound as cool as possible, still being a bird.

"That's why I couldn't find you!" Marcy said, cracking up. "Whoa! You're a bird. That is messed up."

"It's weird, right?" Lance replied.

Marcy helped Walter sit up. He looked around, amazed. More Agency helicopters arrived at the island.

"This is amazing," Walter said. "We did it. We took down the drones, beat the bad guy, saved countless lives. We are so gonna get our jobs back!"

EPILOGUE

"**S**o . . . triple fired," Walter said. He sat on the steps outside the Lincoln Memorial with now-human Lance.

"Yeah, man, that's got to be some kind of record," Lance said.

Walter and Lance fed the pigeons. Lovey, Crazy Eyes, and Jeff were among the flock.

"I really didn't see that coming," Walter said.

"Well, we did break a bunch of laws, and defied orders, and I mean . . . committed a little bit of treason," Lance said.

"Oh right, yeah, the treason. I forgot about the treason," Walter said, bummed.

"Hey, it doesn't matter, man. Look around," Lance said, gesturing. They looked out at the reflecting pond. Everything was safe and sound. People were enjoying the beautiful day.

"Your mother would be so proud of you right now. You kept all those people safe. And you did it your way," Lance said. "But you also did this."

Lance held up a tiny hand and wiggled his fingers.

Walter winced. "Yeah, I'll figure that out. Sorry."

Lance just smiled. "You know, this gluten-free stuff is really starting to grow on me."

"So what do we do now?" Walter asked.

"Oh, we could—" Lance started, but was quickly cut off when two figures wearing ski masks put hoods on both of them. The masked people threw them into an unmarked van. The van peeled off.

In the van, Lance's hood was pulled off, and he looked around. He saw Walter next to him—his head still bagged with soundproof headphones on top. Marcy sitting across from him.

"Marcy?" Lance asked.

With the headphones on, Walter was talking WAY too loudly. "OKAY, I CAN'T SEE OR HEAR, BUT MY OTHER SENSES ARE ELEVATED! SO YOU—" The van took a sharp turn, and Walter smacked into a wall. "OWW!"

Suddenly, Joyless appeared on a screen on

the van's wall. "Agent Sterling. I apologize for the theatrics."

"No, you don't," Lance replied.

"You should've seen your face when we grabbed you," Marcy said.

"I didn't make a face," Lance shot back.

"No one's ever looked more scared," Marcy said.

"Are you two finished?" Joyless asked.

Walter groped around the van. "WE ARE GOING TO BE OKAY, LANCE! USE YOUR BABY HAND TO PICK THE LOCK!"

"Can you please take that off him?" Joyless said.

Marcy yanked the hood off Walter. "Oh, hey— hey, guys. Is this about the treason?"

"Joy, what is going on?" Lance asked, ignoring Walter.

"We realize we were wrong about you," Joyless said. "You're the future of this Agency, and we want you to lead a new team. A highly covert global—"

"Let me stop you right there," Lance said, cutting her off.

He held up his tiny hand to the screen and pointed to Walter.

"I am not leading nothing unless my man Walter is on the team," Lance said.

Marcy leaned in. "Umm, I think she's talking to Walter."

"Oh," Lance said, gesturing to Walter with his tiny hand. "Yeah, yeah, yeah. We, uhhh . . . Sometimes he talk for me, I'll talk for him. Cuz we a team."

"Me?" Walter said.

"We need people like you," Joyless said, smiling. "People who can help the Agency do things a new way. What do you say?"

Walter looked at Lance.

"Looks like we're gonna need some glitter," Lance said.

"Team Weird?" Walter said.

Lance smiled and held out his tiny fist to bump with Walter. "Team Weird."